BEFOR
THE CRY
ENDS

BEFORE
THE CRYING
ENDS

JOHN L. HUGHES

THE BODLEY HEAD
LONDON SYDNEY
TORONTO

To Andrew Sinclair

© John L. Hughes 1977
ISBN 0 370 10612 1
Printed and bound in Great Britain for
The Bodley Head Ltd
9 Bow Street, London WC2E 7AL
by Redwood Burn Ltd,
Trowbridge & Esher
Set in Monotype Imprint
by Gloucester Typesetting Co. Ltd
First published 1977

[1]

There being nothing special much around this town. Not like London nor Paris nor Rome nor Lisbon nor Washington. Not like Cardiff nor Tenby nor Bangor nor plenty of towns you can see anywhere.

No one particular item making you sit up sudden like you never believed what you saw first time off. Not a single special thing for making passing (on to God knows where) strangers remember where they been. No special beauty. No special ugliness. No sudden visions. And no sudden blindness as ever they (them passing strangers) could recall.

Nothing special much around this town for filling empty exiled nights and minds with nostalgia nor things hard to forget a hundred a thousand a hundred thousand miles away. Nothing memorable you understand. No one peculiar thing them passing eyes could retain for ever. No wide gasping geographical statement marked deep across the landscape making them (them passing strangers) whisper all holy:

Only God could have done that.

Now tell me there is no God.

God been poking his fingers up this place.

God definitely done that mountain (or that valley or that cliff or that forest or that sky).

Even the name of this place is forgettable. Pontypridd. A shambles of mystic Welshness. Pontypridd. Something to do with a bridge (there is a bridge). Pontypridd. Something to do with the earth (black stuff). Who could remember such a name? Who could care?

There being nothing special much around this town. Nothing at all. Except perhaps the river. Maybe just that.

The River Taff. Swilling down from Merthyr same as some kind of whip. Dirty candle-coloured by day down through Aberdare Mountain Ash Abercynon and Cilfynydd in a torrent. In a welter of torrents. Grunting sucking lashing whirlpools

5

blackened through by mining trash and coal no man could burn.

Twisting fast down deep inside the guts of Pontypridd. Towards Cardiff. Carrying things. Always carrying things.

Dead terrier. Four headless chickens. Five loaves (from Wonderloaf) and two fish (from Plowman's) floating in circles amid surface scum just off that Marks and Spencer back wall. Two mangled oil cans from Texaco (by way of Halfords) and one sodden *Western Mail* hanging same as nests on the pea-shooter beds fringed haphazard around Ynysangharad Park. And a bucket. And a bugle. And a birthday card. And a trouser leg with the turn-up down. And a boy and his ferret hunting for rats.

Found a bike down there once.

Only needed a chain.

Found a chain down there once.

Only needed a bike.

And in flood that river is mighty. A frightening thing. Unstoppable (if ever man had a mind). Creaking heavy against them quaking banks where houses stand. And people stand. Staring. Up at the rain. Down at the river. Across at each other. Wondering. With tomboys chucking stones snick snick into the grey flow. And today it is raining as last night it rained and the day before. And the night before that day. For this town is Pontypridd. Where they know all about rain.

And it was raining when you got born. And it will be raining when you die. If you die in Pontypridd.

And mister I can tell you for nothing as how when that day comes you will definitely have enough on your plate working your dead mouth on a fiddle into Heaven never mind that hissing rain.

With thoughts like that definitely giving you the willies now and again seeing as how you are not ready for no bloody drop this fair side of three score years and ten. With a stack of functioning left for doing inside your skull not to mention all through your medium rare skin. Leaving them passing strangers to keep on passing by this forgettable place in a gust of wind and rain. On towards London or Paris or Rome or Lisbon or Washington or Cardiff or Tenby or Bangor or anywhere else. For this town is

6

Pontypridd where the gods brought your soul at the beginning of time. And nailed it to a wall.

Walking on sharp down through Taff Street in a December drizzle towards your wife. Towards Woolworth's where Rachel been waiting an hour.

Hello mister high and bloody mighty.

Where the hell you been?

Got held up isn't it.

Pay was late coming.

You smell of drink.

I been here an hour.

Dying for the toilet.

You got some money?

Yes.

For Christ sake Ben.

Giving her forty pounds in your brown envelope hall-marked and stamped with the compliments of the National Coal Board minus the docket away up inside your ratting hat. And watching her run for the Cilfynydd bus jostling through that steaming Christmas crowd like they are litter.

[2]

And shoving heaving on through that steam rising out of hot bodies and wet parkas up Taff Street towards Joe's snooker hall where Mad Ike got this boss-eyed Pole all set up on the pink and black for twelve pounds.

Clocking through the swimming blue murk across them islands of tables. Green baize rectangular islands punctuated here and there by galaxies of red (plenty of red) yellow green brown blue pink and black. And just an arm or a hand or a spider rest cueing off the white into orbit. Chink chink.

Asking Len behind the snack bar for one cheese Hovis and a can of Coke to go with the plate you found on table Number Five.

They been playing two hours.

7

Haydn is holding the pot.

Lot of side betting.

How much start?

Ike give him a black.

Made him break first.

If the Pole gets the pink Ike's gone.

Except the Pole don't get the pink and Ike is not gone. Seeing him grin all wicked as he cues for that pink and cannons it off the black bottom left leaving seven points hanging bottom right.

Ike will take that.

And Ike does. Taking the pot from Haydn nearly before the black settles out of sight. Slipping on his ripped sheepskin and melting back into the fog before the Pole gets crabby. Then there is talk. And the sound of silver and notes.

With that Pole bragging it around as how he is not on form and as how Mad Ike been talking him off and all the rest of his sour crap. Being lies all lies and a fat figment of his Polish imagination. With Mad Ike being the best thing you ever saw behind a cue around this place since you was a snotgobbling whelp not tall enough to pot proper.

Mad Ike talk me off.

Mad Ike a cheating bastard.

Mad Ike he should be banned from this place.

Mad Ike he no good without his mouth.

He take free ball when no free ball.

I never play the bastard no more.

Mad Ike no good.

But he is good. And they all listen quiet. And they know he is good. And they have seen and heard it all before. For each man there is an authority on Mad Ike and the way it is with his game. Being cut regular on sixty breaks and the hundred last winter which made him a saint. Telling Len

Ike must be getting on.

Fifty-five.

His eyes are going.

Why don't he wear glasses?

He could wear glasses.

Proud.

Ike don't want no glasses.

He got pride.

I don't bet on him no more.

Plenty do.

That will stop.

One day Ben he might take a black start.

One day you might give him that.

Not me mister.

Not for money.

No not for money.

You don't want that.

But you might give him a black.

With Haydn crossing to the bar and buying twenty Embassy Mild out of the three pounds he made on Ike. Making you wonder about them wore-out eyes he supposed to have and knowing bloody right as how you will have white whiskers down to your manhood before ever you see him off with a seven-point start. Go ask that coughing knot of shadows. Go ask the Pole. And for every voice answering yes you call out liar just as loud. Never mind where the betting went mister. Go ask Haydn. Go ask Ike.

With Joe's gone quiet now same as some kind of woman out from orgasm. Staring through her windows drizzle-flecked under that darkening sky down into Taff Street where Ike puts up his collar. And getting on home will sleep the sleep of the proud. Feeling this nudge at your elbow. Seeing Haydn lock away Ike's cue.

Saw your brother Lew this morning.

Off work again.

He don't work much do he?

Same as you.

I got ulcers.

Big as lemons.

Work could burst them.

On the sick isn't it.

I got these tablets.

Smarties.

What you mean Smarties?

These is tablets.

Smarties is different colours.

Not all bloody yellow.

See it don't say Smarties.

Lew said to tell you.

What?

Look in on him.

And his wife and kid.

Lovely woman that nigger.

Lovely wife.

We don't bother much.

He's your brother isn't it.

Brothers should bother.

I only got sisters.

I know.

Wish I had a nigger wife.

Fancy a nigger woman now and then.

They got pretty names.

Same as Lew's wife.

Melody.

That's a pretty name.

Wish I had a wife called Melody.

Wish I had a nigger woman.

They got the skin isn't it.

Staring down again across at Mothercare blocked full of bright-lit caring mothers twice three four or five times over till caring have become some kind of tired habit far beyond the call of instinct. Who knows about instinct? Who wants to be a mother?

I'm expecting.

Poor bitch.

I want my baby.

Wait till you got five.

I don't want five.

Just the two.

Boy and girl.

Boy the eldest.

Just the two.
All I want.
>And me.
>And bloody me.
>All that central heating.
>Gets him worked up.
>Expecting my sixth.
What do you want?
>An easy time.
They say the first is bad.
>They are all bad.
>Samantha was the worst.
>Number three.
Number three?
>Thought I'd die.
>Wanted to.
>Days in labour.
>Wanted to.
Days?
>And nights.
>Never forget number three.
Samantha.
>Hateful little cat.
>Never had no looks on her.
>Not after the way it was.

Hearing Saint Catherine gonging out six o'clock across Ponty-
pridd where the streets begin to empty and the buses begin to
fill. Double-decker single-decker cream and blue red and white
(from Aberdare) booming out exhaust noise throaty lazy fat diesel
sounds and blueness and poison the property of Taff Ely Council.
Hearing Haydn telling you again and again and again
What shall I tell him then?
>Who?
Lew.
You got a message?
>No message.
And leaving Joe's with this chill over your legs warming off as

you trot through Ynysangharad Park up the river path towards the
shadows of the baths locked tight and vandalised till May. And
dropping to a walk staring down at the surging black Taff picked
out silver now and then with ghost lights and neon from Woolworth's and the Maypole and Dewhurst's and Tesco's giving that
monster speed.

I never said for certain.

I never said definite.

Thank God you come Ben.

I love you.

I been out of my mind.

No word for a week.

I love you.

I love you.

    I love you.

O I love you Ben.

Christ help me.

I been in pain for you.

I adore you.

I don't eat nothing.

I just sit around waiting.

Waiting like a dummy.

I love you sick.

O Ben.

    I love you.

    O Melody.

[3]

And she have undone your donkey jacket easy never mind the
rain getting in ice cold where she opened up them buttons.

Holding in close. Pressing you tight against the baths wall.
Feeling her shiver there in the dark till she sucks some warmth
away from your body. Stretching up her face to kiss your neck.
Her wet chilled cheeks moving to a smile you cannot see as you

wrap her in closer. Nudging those lips towards yours. And making those lips wait as they part eager breathing quick for kissing. And this small sound coming from those lips making you brush them with your own. And holding her face in your hands which got deadened by work long ago. Feeling nothing much except the feel of their own hard skin. And the softness of hers. They feel her skin. And letting your two mouths meet damp and warm till you are numb and electrified half out of your skull. And wanting that.

With her pulling away sudden like she got to or die. And stroking your face. And staring. And staring and searching. And full of sad happy tears running mingling with that drizzle. And groaning in to kiss again. And again. And again till you think she will hurt her breasts from the pressing. And feeling her breathless.

Damn you.

Holding her gentle with one arm. Turning her half away. Letting her feel under your shirt for the heat of your flesh.

There is no end to this.

I must be with you.

I feel so awful.

I go out of my mind.

O I love you Ben.

Being the way it is with you and Melody. And the way it have been for over one year since that night out East Glamorgan casualty when Lew got took in half-dead from this hiding Ivor and his opos give him for sleeping in the wrong bed. At the wrong time. With the wrong woman.

Glad you came Ben.

Police was here.

    Left a message at the pit.

    I was washing.

    Just come up.

    Afternoons.

They asked about family.

Told them you was in the pit.

Routine I think.

    Lew will mend.

13

Fractured skull.

He got colour.

Always a good sign.

See his colour?

He's a bastard.

A right bastard.

You know that?

You love him.

I did once.

Once I loved him a lot.

I been hurt too much.

This is his scene.

I can't stand it no more.

Now we just live together.

I know the feeling.

With the two of you staring at Lew through till the early hours. And Melody crying now and again very quiet same as anybody who got a screwed gut being terrible upset by the entire bloody mess.

You got a child.

A little girl.

Miriam.

Handicapped.

I know.

With that little darkie staff nurse coming and going fixing Lew's plasma drip and pumping his arm with this pulser bulb. Wiping off his sweat and charting him on some kind of progress graph hanging clipped above the bed. Seeing them small dots level off across the sheet and knowing the worst is over. And knowing as how somewhere out in the great blue yonder your brother got this massive prayer going for him in all the right places with a host of angels not to mention clouds full of assorted holies standing guard above his soul seeing he don't march off premature before his number is rolled out on that golden heavenly carpet. Being lies all lies at the end of the matter. Being just the way luck runs for Lew.

Clocking Melody there sucking long drags out of her Number

Six staring up at the graph and seeing her loveliness hiding deep behind them drawn cheeks. Shaking back her midnight hair. Sighing pained on a bitter frown.

I can take you home.

If you want that Melody.

If you like.

And her standing up slow same as a zombie. Worn out. Waiting for that world to knock her about some more.

I got a car.

And you take hold of her hand. And you feel them fingers tighten on your palm. A girl feel. A woman feel. A big feel of chemistry. A body contact you never had with her before. Flesh against flesh. Just hands. Nothing more than hands touching. And they cannot let go. They cannot. Not even through the disinfectant scent of four or five or five hundred corridors. Across the soggy rolling lawns. Past light past dark past sound past silence. They cannot let go. Touching each other. You want that. You keep wanting that. You cannot let go.

And at the car she kisses your hand. Making you look into her face where them eyes don't cry no more. Where them eyes pull your own with signals with messages with fear you cannot bear to understand.

You listen to me.

I'm taking you home.

The best thing.

The only thing.

I want you.

Christ.

Bloody hell.

I know.

O I know.

With this drumming feeling of trespass all bunched nasty in the front of your mind. With this long low ache of violation bent bow-shaped through your insides. With them thinking valves clogged good and thick same as boozing for hours. Except you have definitely not boozed lately. And knowing as how no drink you ever took have laid you down so helpless in your brain.

15

And her body is thawed now against your own. Holding her tight. Possessive. Listening eyes closed to the wind noises snittering through the conifers bordering the baths. Feeling deceitful to the world but honest with each other. A private feeling. A shared agony. An ecstasy. A wrongness. And a love.

Will I see you tomorrow?

I been praying you are not on afternoons.

Say your are on nights.

Please God say you are.

I been working it out.

    I'm on nights.

I love you.

I love you.

    Tomorrow.

    On the hill.

Our hill.

Our lovely hill.

    I might bring you a present.

I might let you give it to me.

And she is gone. And you don't question it. For you have learned not to say good-bye. Not to say hello. Nor any other words that waste the time you got when one day is worth a week. When one hour is worth a day. When one minute is worth an hour. When one second is worth a kiss.

[4]

There being nothing better designed nor nothing more deliberate forged by wickedness (as ever you have come across) for making grown men yearn genuine to be little boys again than night-shift down at the Deep Maritime. The very sight of her silhouetted winding gear clawing upwards grasping at a frozen moon laying mighty claim to ownership of things way beyond this earth can chill your soul when the wind is right.

And you have seen some of them grown men kitted out for

work with full bellies and number one physical stop at her gates. You have seen them stop rooted to the hard ground fear sweating from their pores with flickering frightened eyes staring at the sight of her. Premonition gripping icy round them grown men throats and whispers from that Reaper telling them to turn and head for home. And they do. Some of them. But for every man who turns away a hundred pass on stupid (with you being stupid regular around this place) down into her great digestion easing out the coal she have grown inside that fertile womb.

I'm not going down there again.

Not for a sack of effing tea.

Too much bloody water.

Cowing river down there.

Up to my knackers all night.

I got cowing gills growing.

Eff it I say.

I'm not going down there again.

But they do. The stupid ones. The ones who pretend they got guts. The hard men. Same as yourself. Solid bone from the neck up. The ones they call colliers. You should see them when they die.

Going through to number five lamp room with the rest of your section. Shivering coughing yawning breaking wind and the stink of Welsh Brewers everywhere. Picking up your disc and grafting kit while Ernie Smallman pegs his bingo board counting off the moles as they wriggle past.

Three eight four C.

Beano's gang right?

    Right.

Cold night.

There's ice on your district.

They been firing all afternoon.

No sweat Ben.

Easy shift.

    More muck than coal.

Crossing the frost-bitten yard and walking up the tramlines in a herd towards the cages where you are frisked for fags and matches before they pin you inside. With fifteen of you jammed together staring out at the moon. And the oil-soaked gates slammed shut at your staring faces. Number five section. Beano's gang ready for dropping out of sight beneath that slumbering world.

Shooting down the shaft sudden like. Leaving your guts on the pithead same as usual. Steadying yourselves against each other. Blowing hard through your nostrils. Feeling the pop pop inside your ears clearing them drums. Letting in the noise. Dropping deeper down into the cold with that cage bulb blowing half-way like it always does when Belsen is winding.

That's Belsen that is.

Mad Polish sod.

He have gone to the bogs.

Forgot about us.

Sitting there I expect.

Reading the *Sketch*.

Except Belsen is not in the bogs (thank God). Hearing them cables whine above your head as the whole thing slows down. Feeling this icy updraught and catching your breath with the chill from it whooshing past. And braking to a stop same as a gentle thump under your feet.

Switching on your lamps though there is plenty of light. And tramping like some kind of retreating platoon now four abreast hobnailed onto the loco where you sit down in a skiff shivering alongside one-eyed Ivor chewing at his twist gobbing out the juice between his boots. Being this filthy habit he got and dirtier than yourself who gobs to the left in consideration of others.

Where was you last night?

Missed a bloody good night.

Rachel was there.

    Likes the rugby club.

    Likes a laugh.

Where was you Ben?

    Down Hensol Castle.

    Never got back till late.

Rachel said something.

Visiting the kid isn't it.
She said something.
Hell of a case.
Likes a laugh.
   She been acting up.
   Miriam.
   Had to have electrics.
How long they keeping her?
   For ever.
Jesus.
That's long.
   Brain damage.
   Keep draining her head.
   Hydrocephalic.
   They got to do it regular.
Rachel never went.
   Don't want to know.
You got your work cut out.
   No sweat.
   Good place Hensol.
   Good staff.
   Know what they are on.
Got to isn't it.
I heard about Hensol.
You got to know what you are on.
Eff that for a lark.
   No sweat.
   No lark.
With that loco rattling on through the mile-end tunnel taking you to the face. Feeling this sway setting up as the line arcs towards number three district closed permanent in honour (they say) of Ned and Sidney who was pulped there last September when the roof fell in. Being lies all lies at the end of the matter and just something to tell to the living. With the coal faced out and finished a week before they died. Go ask them souls of Ned and Sidney.
   Mad Ike took her home.

Making you stare at him like he is pig muck. Being the way you think of Ivor regular. And he don't look at you with his one eye. And he don't smile one bit. Telling you them tales between gobbing out his twist juice all over the place.

Took her home.

Mad Ike.

Who?

Mad Ike.

He took Rachel home.

Last night.

Where was you?

Sleeping.

What do you mean?

Just saying isn't it.

Must have been late.

They was walking.

Must have been late.

Not so late.

How do you know?

You was sleeping.

I know.

She never come late.

Rachel is all right.

Just saying isn't it.

Mad Ike took her home.

Just a passing remark.

You got a dirty mind Ivor.

Anybody ever tell you that?

Plenty of people.

They are all wrong.

Clacking on inside that skiff. Settling lower as the roof shortens. Passing brown rock facings dripping oozing running at an angle on account of the gradient. With that loco picking up a lick taking you down deeper into your district where the chill bites sharper and the ice splinters sparkle all along the ceiling arch.

I don't want it.

I don't bloody want it.

I been taking tablets.
　　What kind of tablets?
Antibiotics.
And Codeines.
I took a lot.
Thought I was dying.
　　You could have killed yourself.
　　Silly cow.
　　You know that Rachel?
I don't bloody want it.
　　Tablets is no good isn't it.
　　You got to get the thing drained.
　　There's plenty do that.
My mother won't let me.
　　She got to.
She says to have it.
　　Have it?
And you got to marry me.
She hid all the bloody Codeines.
　　How old are you?
Eighteen.
Next birthday.
If it gets born.
By the time that happens.
I should be eighteen.
　　Christ.
I tried him.
He don't want to know.
He never heard of me.
Flush off little girl.
You are not on my books.
Reckoning as how no amount of praying to that Lord up there is going to take the edge off your problem. With Rachel being six weeks overdue buying her ticket ready for the nuthouse not to mention yourself in sympathy for certain on that affliction. Running her hard one January night from Cilfynydd down Norton Bridge through Trallwn till she is dropping knackered outside

21

them Ynysangharad Park gates. Pulling her frantic through the loosened mesh and down to the river bank where you tell her

Get in.

What?

Get in.

Get in the water.

O Christ no Ben.

Don't you even like me?

I thought you liked me a bit.

I'm not doing it.

O Christ no Ben.

For the baby.

You silly bitch.

It's for the baby.

Kill the baby.

Not you Rachel.

I got no breath.

I'm holding you.

Get in.

What about the rats?

I seen rats down here.

O Christ no Ben.

O Christ no.

There's no rats.

Not in the winter.

You are a bloody liar.

My brother goes ratting.

He got ferrets.

There's plenty of rats.

Not at this time of night.

Get in.

The water will do it.

Shoving Rachel into that wicked Taff up to her knees so she screams at the cold. And screams at you hitching up her skirt and crying and howling same as a little girl.

Seeing her sit right down or stumble on the river bed till that water have risen over her hips. Cutting off her bawling and the rest pretty damn quick. And you got her cold hand tight (a weak girl) feeling this slow strong tug of the current wanting to send her down as far as the sea. And her baby. And you (if you give it half a chance). Feeling cramp coming from your elbow down. And knowing she could get washed away easy if them fingers fail. And they do. And she is gone from sight without one single sound. All in one gasp. Scaring you good.

Running racing pelting headlong through the long grass and pea-shooter beds same as some kind of epileptic rhino with piles. Keeping up alongside the flow. Alongside the drift which took her out of sight. Staring wide-eyed watery in the rising wind across where she should be. Seeing one head two heads three heads more. Flicking up and down in the drizzle murk. But none of them are hers.

Ben O Ben.

Get me Ben.

Get me out.

Where?

Rachel.

Rachel.

In the river.

I know.

Where?

And an arm rising just for a second. Just a flash of it. Same as some kind of black branch picked out against Woolworth's wall. Telling you where. Jumping in thinking the water is over your head. Finding out it is up to your knees. And slipping (same as Rachel) twisting splashing on over the river bed trash. Wading frightened deeper to where she is. Feeling for her. Groping blind. Touching the soft squash of skin in a frantic clutch. Pulling her upright with the strength of five men.

That should fix it.

Mam will kill me.

She'll bloody kill me.

Tell her straight.

What?

You been out in the rain.

Tell her straight.

You tell her that.

Getting your cold bones jolted hard as the skiff stops. Hearing talk and laughter somewhere down there. And the hum of that loco running smooth in neutral waiting for you to scuttle off in a stoop. And you do. Beano's gang. Single file under the five-foot ceiling going down to four foot four (in twelve district you got to work in two foot nine). Walking funny like Groucho Marx up to your face section.

Switch the belt on.

Test the power.

Got to have power.

Where's the cowing power?

Kick the red button.

Now press the green.

And the clogged crunch of that conveyor chattering awkward while it clears. Shuddering through the whole cutback till it settles rolling rubbery ready for loading.

Shift the cack first.

This is your captain speaking.

Load the cack.

Clocking Ivor peel off naked to his waist same as usual never mind the ice. Showing tattoos carved blue and red in love hearts linked by arrows with the name of Eva. Being this Jewish piece you seen plenty of times. Eva. Flogging handbags in Ponty market. With her not giving half a wank for his one-eyed chances. Letting him help her on Saturdays and Wednesdays when he is on nights or mornings or absent.

Working in a line filling that belt with cack and ice till the seam is clear. Throwing off the shivers shovel for shovel alongside Beano. Getting blacker hour by hour and watching them faces streak ugly same as yourself with sweat.

You tell Mad Ike.

Give him the word.

When you see him Ivor.

You tell him.

Keep away from Rachel.

Keep away from her.

And on Paradise Hill the rain have stopped or not yet started. Walking on up past Glyntaff cemetery (still asleep having missed that second coming by miles) with a feel under your feet like the feel of wet foam Dunlopillo instead of grass. Squeaking sideways across that slope. Fouling the soles of your fell boots so they don't grip no more. Slipping upwards at an angle. Slipping squeaking wetting your knees. Panting (a cough now and then) hearing the sound of your own breath and knowing the coal dust have made this small start inside them heaving lungs. Not liking that.

Till you reach the hardcore path running rugged between six good oaks and an elm. Taking any wanderer straight across the hill into Cilfynydd and on past Jake's dump where all this scrap iron waits for collection once a year. Being nearly a mile off from where you normally stand waiting for Melody. Where the oak trees give plenty of shelter. Where the shadows are always thick.

And you are early by half an hour staring out through the leaf-shed trees across Pontypridd. Making you think as how (from Paradise Hill) that town is everywhere your eyes can look. Hanging down in terraced layers same as stripes drawn by a child. From the Graig over towards Treforest cut deliberate into halves by Stow Hill Road with that cream-painted Central School perched on top. Clear as crystal this winter morning. Rising high and catching the sun. And the sun catching Graigwen above Pwllgwaun (where you was born) all in an eighteen-carat light. With the Vee of that Rhondda Valley rebellious misting up beyond and blowing rain. Wetting Paradise Hill again. Washing out the vision from inside your wondering mind. Who cares about a vision? Who knows about a mind?

With half-past eight coming and going bringing heavier rain like there will be no tomorrow. Soaking your donkey jacket this darker shade of blue. Shivering you. Making you move about under them oaks. Feeling this nearly empty Chipsticks bag in

25

your pocket from a week ago. Finishing the crumbs with a swallow and a sigh. Reminding you that to be hungry is to be colder never mind the mystery of love. And Melody is very late.

Why are you standing there O my lamb?

    I am waiting for Melody O my Lord.

    She have promised to come.

You are a soft bugger O my lamb.

    Why is that Lord?

She have forgot isn't it.

    No way Lord.

    She loves me.

How do you know?

    She said.

And do you love her O my lamb?

    Yes Lord.

How do you know?

    I told her isn't it.

    And there's this feeling.

Guts ache O my lamb.

You are a soft bugger.

She is your brother's wife.

    That don't matter Lord.

    Not when you are in love.

Who been telling you that O my lamb?

    In the Bible Lord.

    Faith hope and love.

    And the greatest of these is love.

    They are gifts.

Knickers O my lamb.

Love is guts ache.

And a bit of fun.

    We don't have fun Lord.

    Melody and me.

    We are serious.

A sad fact.

    She been thinking about leaving Lew.

    I been thinking about leaving Rachel.

26

We want to live with each other.
Melody and me.
We been thinking.
She will hurt Lew.
You will hurt Rachel.
The kids will get hurt.
Everybody gets pain.
All because of your guts ache.
The greatest is love.
I seen it written.
In your Bible.
When I was little.
I never wrote that O my lamb.
It don't say I wrote that book.
It is not in the front.
No.
Men wrote it.
The way they wanted to.
And when they got stuck
(with all that thinking)
they blamed me isn't it.
Love is guts ache.
I'm telling you Ben.
And a bit of fun.
My words O lamb.
From another book.
They are written there.
In my hand.
Where is that book?
I don't believe you got no book.
Where is it Lord?
Up here O my lamb.
You will see.
When Lord?
When you die O my lamb.
You got to kick it first.
It is a privilege.

27

And Melody is there. And she did not forget. Being lies all lies from the mouth of that Lord taking advantage of the cold and the wind and the rain. Catching you lonely after night shift down the Deep Maritime. Playing poker for your soul. Kissing her gentle. Kissing her long.

I been to the surgery.

Lew got pneumonia.

Just a touch.

I had to go.

    Too much beer.

    He got a beer chill.

    I love you.

I love you.

Just seeing you.

O I love you.

    You want that present?

O all night.

I been longing.

I was sick with longing.

I love you.

I love you.

And I come on.

I bloody come on.

    What?

[6]

There is this packet of big trouble walking silent through the streets of Cilfynydd (and up and down the back lanes) at nearly any time of day or night no matter what the weather. Walking slow proud deliberate and arrogant. Clocking that kingdom with a bright blue stare. Freezing into cowardice the spirits of all but the bravest most rebellious mutineers. From Ann Street down through William Street past the chip shop in Jones Street up Mary Street into Wood Street (passing his house) and on up the slope towards Oaklands by the Spar shop where he been known to catch the return bus back again as far as the main road.

Going by the name of Duke. And when his mood is right (or wrong) he is instant death. If you was born a dog or a cat. If you was born a rabbit or a hare or a rat (especially if you was born a rat). Duke. Being white and brown but mostly white. Duke is an executioner. Duke is a lurcher.

Five dogs (dead).

Three cats (dead).

One sheep (missing).

Eighteen rabbits (dead).

Two hares (dead).

Seventy-four rats (dead).

With Duke being a lethal whip of sinew muscle courage and teeth. A killer thriving on killing. And mister I can tell you for nothing as how that animal never took one prisoner in six years of life (and death). He don't know nothing about begging for a bone. Nor chasing some rubber ball. Nor Lassie meaty chunks. Nor canine neurotics. Nor vets. Nor walkies in the park. Duke only knows about killing. And his knowledge is complete.

So if ever you was to ask who might be the owner of that lurcher they would have to tell you Beano. At any rate it was definitely Beano who bought Duke his first licence (not to mention his last) a few years back out of plain respect for them police officers threatening to do him for twenty pounds otherwise.

And at half-past four Beano is calling for you with Duke and three ferrets by the names of Eenie Meenie and Mynee (a rat got Mo back in October). With Rachel all irritable around the kitchen like her drawers is full of holly.

Thought you was sleeping till six.

You got no colour.

    I forgot about Beano.

    There's rats up the allotment.

    I promised him.

There's always rats.

    Not nesting.

    These are nesting.

Brian lost a pigeon Tuesday night.

He got traps set.

Bloody rats.

Cilfynydd is a rat hole.

It's the tips.

They breed up there.

You got to have rats.

If you got tips.

You said I could come.

When?

Come what?

Ratting.

The next time you said.

You said I could come.

Do you want to come?

I never been ratting.

Nobody ever took me ratting.

I want to see.

All right Rachel.

I don't mind.

You can hold the dog.

You got to take care.

Seeing the black and white of Brian's pigeon cote looming up through the fading light as you edge downwind in a curve across them half-dug furrows running random through the allotments. With Beano casting his torch beam here and there on and off searching for the traps he have set (being cage traps) catching them vermin alive and scratching. Hearing this rattle nearby same as some kid running a stick across a mesh fence and knowing there is a trap with a rat inside. Hearing the rattle stop as your vibrations scare that creature into stiffness.

Jesus.

Look at that.

With Beano flooding the trap in his beam. And pulling back the strangle grass from over the whole thing. Hearing Rachel gasp at your side clutching her mouth to cut off her noise. And Duke whining shivering staring making as if to dig with his front paws.

Knowing what it is that he can see. Knowing he got no business barking till Beano tells him what to do.

And that brown rat never ate the bacon bait still hanging on its lure central inside the trap being more bothered by escape than feeding. And you never knew a rat yet who would eat his bacon once he got trapped. With this one being medium large looking like a female judging by the streamline from nose to shoulders. And getting highly agitated squeaking spitting snarling with that dead empty quiet habit they take on after smelling Duke.

What we got then Duke?

Rats Duke rats.

Go find them boy.

Go dig them rats.

Rats rats rats.

And Rachel lets him go off the cord away just to the left under the raised floor of the pigeon cote where he starts barking and digging like a fury inane.

He got the nest Beano.

Like a sieve under here.

Lay boy.

Good dog.

Sit Duke.

You need ferrets.

Seeing Rachel come towards you picking like a fairy through the grass holding her skirt close to her legs. Clocking big eyes at the hole Duke have dug and about eight or nine tunnel runs cross-sectioned. With no rats in sight nor sound except the one Beano have taken from the trap and is holding round the neck in a tight gloved grip. Giving you the willies. Wondering how Beano got brought up in the first place.

And Beano shoves his rat down a hole. Pulling Eenie from inside his shirt (with Meenie and Mynee poking out their arrow heads all inquisitive) so he can follow down quick. Hearing this terrified squealing all over under the ground where you are standing. Letting the other two ferrets slip down different holes. And Duke going frantic casting about excited everywhere. Barking savage and whining in between his barks. With Beano telling Rachel

You better stand off.

They will fly out.

Get hold of this lamp.

The ferrets is facing them now.

Wait till they strike.

They will come out flying.

And they strike. And the grass is alive with brown rats as they come shooting out of them holes away from the ferrets same as screaming bullets. Kicking one off your leg. Hearing Rachel scream frantic and Beano laughing. Seeing her drop that lamp and run in circles.

Oof O bloody hell.

You never said.

Oof I could kill you.

Ooh Ooh you bastards.

Watching Duke work. Seeing him catch this fat bull in mid air like it is a bat. Shaking all hell out of the thing. Pawing it to the ground. Taking off the head in one snap. And twisting and nosing through the strangle grass till he finds another travelling. Getting them teeth into it wriggling screaming showing this snow white underside through the gloom. Shaking shaking rattling their bones. Breaking their backs. Using that lurcher head same as a swordsman uses his foil. Until there is no more squealing except from Rachel swearing she got bit in the leg.

Clocking Beano enticing Eenie Meenie and Mynee from the rat runs blocked with dead or dying. Seeing them go for his bacon pieces (a separate piece for Meenie on account of him only going for smoked) and back inside his shirt. Taking a count and counting seven over the grass. And Duke flopped on his belly all of a pant with his jaws dripping from froth and blood.

Better get that leg fixed Rachel.

Just a nip.

It don't hurt.

Poisonous.

Better see to it.

Could turn you into a rat.

And out in East Glamorgan casualty this child Pakistani doctor gets some practice with his needle pumping Rachel full of penicillin and streptomycin just in case. With that just in case being Weil's Disease you seen once on Beano after he got chewed by Mo. Keeping him out in Ward Ten for three weeks at the very least not to mention big jabs every four or five hours night and day to stop him going bananas.

With all that stuff making Rachel puke over the floor of your Avenger driving back on Upper Boat roundabout. Being handy for the pub set off secret to the left. Telling Rachel

You need Smirnoff and lime.

Settle your guts.

    I got more to come up.

The drugs have done it.

Better sick than sorry.

Rats is very nasty.

I said be careful.

Pulling to a stop outside the *Upper Boat Inn* and noticing what lovely dark eyes she got all of a sudden. With them eyes staring at you pathetic in the ghostly pale of her drained face.

You don't know bloody nothing Ben.

You don't know bloody nothing.

Seeing tears well up glittering around them lovely eyes. And spilling in a trickle down past her nose. Reckoning as how that puking must have upset her more than you thought.

Vodka will settle it.

You are OK Rachel.

I had jabs myself.

It wears off.

    What I got don't ever wear off.

    You don't know bloody nothing.

Is that right?

    I got a baby inside me.

    I got to do it over again.

    I think I would rather die.

    You don't know nothing.

So it is Saturday morning and you are playing Haydn for the cost of the table. With Joe's being hardly awake yet judging by the feel of the place and six tables still covered by them grubby fawn dust drapes. Stepping careful out of the way of Len's brush. Seeing him sweep up this pile of dog ends left over from the night before around Table Seven (being favourite for big-money play on account of the fast baize and bouncing cushions making duff shots cost). And you can only count four others cueing in the entire hall. With the air you are breathing being clean and strange and funny.

Watching Haydn light an Embassy Gold from a Senior Service match booklet. And dropping his spent booklet into Len's dog-ends.

Sloppy bastard.

Like that at home?

> This is home.

> Flush off Len.

And Len flushes off grinning as Haydn lines up for the blue hanging bottom right. And misses. And goes in off the black. Marking up another seven for yourself bringing that marker eighteen points ahead. Catching the white Haydn rolls back to baulk. Telling him

You need a snooker to win.

And pockets a foot wide.

Potting that blue sweet as sugar but messing up on position for the pink. And playing safety sending your white back down behind the line.

I got no chance Ben.

I need two snookers.

> And the pink and black.

And the pink and black.

No chance there.

Clocking Haydn still bent staring at the pink. Then at the black.

Then in a walking stoop round and round the white same as a contortionist. Crouching down on his haunches holding the cush with one hand. Staring eye level along the line of that white to pink. Steadying himself with the cue upright in the other hand same as some kind of midget Moses looking for flaws in the Lord's stony commandments. With that Lord telling him

Thou shalt not pot. For if thou pottest the pink in thy left-hand corner pocket thou shalt go in off bottom right. But if thou dost not pot the pink then thou shalt not go in off but thou shalt leave thine opponent with a straight six shot somewhere as sure as I madest little green apples O my cock-eyed lamb.

And Haydn is all ears for that good Lord. Playing safe at the end of the problem. Fluke shooting the white behind the black still on the spot.

I'm playing safe isn't it.

I got no chance.

You need bigger balls.

Shooting at the pink grateful to knock it any shape. And leaving Haydn with a hanging shot middle left.

That's hanging.

I got no chance.

Seeing him play safe again. Clocking him lean right across the table so both his short legs are off the floor. But letting that foul pass on account of the score. Noticing he got one grey sock and one blue longer than the other. With the heels nearly gone on them dusty brogues. Making you wonder about ulcers and the way it is living on assistance.

Big fight last night.

Lew and his wife.

Hit hell out of her.

Might have broke her leg.

That's the talk.

Feeling your colour go like somebody just pulled the plug on all your blood. And in the first instant the feeling is the feeling of fear.

Taking your shot mechanical. Staring at him half-numb as he measures up his play. Watching him grope for the rest under the table all earnest looking. Amazed he is so determined being so far behind and nothing but pennies on the game. Letting your mind get eaten alive with the question Why? And answering that Lew have found out about you and Melody. And that he is probably searching the town for you right now. And that he have been up Cilfynydd and told Rachel. And how she must be feeling with a lump inside her gut. And a thing like you coming home to her. If ever you reach home again which you will definitely not once Lew gets a hold of your shaking skin. And the first feeling of fear is fear for your life. Making you clean forget about how you love Melody. And the secret things you have told each other in a hundred dark corners and lonely places.

When he is lying there on top of me
I pretend it is you.
When I kiss his lips
I pretend they are yours.
Everything is ugly
without you.
  The other night in bed
  I nearly called her Melody.
  I nearly said your name.
I resent her having you.
I die when I think of it.
I want to be her body.
  The thought of him and you.
  Just the thought of that.
It is pain to think.
Thinking is a dead end.
When we are together
there is only us.
  No one else exists.
  They have not been born.
  We must live a dream.
Just us O my love.
  Just us.

Being lies all lies in the cold light of Joe's. With Haydn wiping his nose on that National Assistance sleeve he had given to him from a chapel jumble. And Saint Catherine gonging out ten o'clock like it is the first hour of Domesday come.

And he snicks that pink so careful it is like a caress. More of a suggestion than a shot. A whispered magic sending you into a snooker behind the black. Seeing him stand back proud with what he done. Sucking in this long drag from his cigarette and chalking that tip all confident.

Something to do with money.

They was shouting about money.

Her and him.

> Was they?

Always about money isn't it.

That's how it starts.

I've had some.

Always gets around to money.

> How do you know Haydn?
> Was you there?

Live opposite don't I?

Can't help hearing.

You seen him?

> We don't bother much.

You was saying.

You ought to go isn't it.

Keep in touch.

He's your brother.

Christmas next week.

> I might.
> I think I might.

Good thing.

> How is the woman?
> You said she was hurt.

Fell downstairs.

May have pushed her.

Hell of a row.

Who can tell?

So it don't have nothing to do with you thank God. Feeling that colour coming back gradual till you are almost holding a

37

steady cue. Letting your mind shrug off them frightened feelings but cocking up that snooker missing the pink by a foot. Knowing you must go to her. Knowing you have tenderness to give. And comfort for her body. Her lovely body violated by a different man. Hurt by his hand. Her gentleness spoiled by some desperate trespass way beyond any laws you don't want to know. Being the second instant. Making you think now not of yourself.

With Haydn nearly dancing around after your white waiting for it to settle. Willing the thing to keep rolling back down the table till it nestles nasty (for you) behind the black. And him squatting right on his haunches looking squint-eyed nose level with the cush along his white to pink line. Hearing him squeak all excited.

Free ball.

You got to give me that.

I got a free ball.

    You can hit the pink.

Not both sides.

I got no chance.

No chance there.

I want a free ball.

Go on ask Len.

That's a free ball.

Definitely fouled.

I want a free ball.

    Take a free ball.

Seeing he have marked up his six putting him seventeen behind and a bit of progress on his game needing just one snooker apart from the pink and black. Sending the soft sod into some kind of rapture he can hardly contain as he lets his cue breathe the white up against the black.

That's dirty Haydn.

    It don't matter.

    I got no chance.

You are bloody right.

Not bothering to play out careful. Knocking the black all shapes to the far end of the table and back again leaving the pink on a long shot for Haydn top left. And he pots it clean as soap.

All on the black Ben.

I took you to the black.

> You played good.

> See if you can win.

I got no chance.

They took her to hospital.

> What?

The nigger girl.

Had the ambulance.

They took her in.

Passing him the long spider even before he begins to reach for it. Noticing he is all of a quiver. Noticing him examine the tip end on that long cue. Making a fuss about the leather being shiny and how the hell do Len earn his money if he don't maintain the equipment. And Len not hearing on purpose. Turning up his radio so the hall knows Slade is wishing *Merry Christmas Everybody*. Watching Haydn go through the ritual of roughing the tip on that spider cue with his penknife. And chalking the thing respectful like his fingers is holding a virgin's nipple.

I got no chance.

You want a pound on the black?

> Yes.

And the two of you handing Len a pound each for the pot being anybody's guess who will sink the black. Except you have lost your confidence and your interest in the game. Knowing deep down as how Haydn must win unless you get lucky. Not caring about the future of that pound anyway with the poor sod looking like he can find good use for the money providing he walks quick past them betting shops and don't remember about Spotform in the *Daily Mirror*.

They brought her back though.

Never kept her out there.

X-rays I expect.

Funny things legs.

> Might be broke.

39

Lovely pair of legs.
The nigger girl.
    Melody.
Lovely.
They got the legs isn't it.
Pity if she broke one.
Give her a limp.
    Might have sprained it.
    She could have done that.
They had an ambulance.
Took her out.
Brought her back.
Broke her leg.
X-rays I expect.
Broke it.
That's the talk.
Chucked her downstairs.
Your brother chucked her flying.
She cut his face nasty.
Must have clawed his face.

Feeling this chill around your shoulders though Len have shut
the windows. Reckoning that shiver must be the willies or fear or
something from thinking about Melody getting thumped by Lew
and the sad effect his fists got on flesh and bone. Being there right
now in your mind. On the top of that stairway watching them
fight. Seeing her claw out at his face. Being driven desperate to
do that. And him chucking her about the place. Punching her.
Throwing her down into the passage. And hearing that cue ball
chink. And seeing Haydn pot the black.

You want another game?
You got time for three reds?
Double or quits if you like.
I was lucky.
I got no chance.

Watching him take two pounds from Len and shove them into
his back pocket marked out oblong where he keeps his fags. And
he is smiling like a nun who just been wicked again. Putting on

40

his filthy little denim jacket and stretching himself wide same as a labourer who just done a day's work earning his wages. Being sort of the same thing as far as Haydn is concerned.

Three reds Ben?

Double or quits?

Not today Haydn.

You are too good.

I'm on form isn't it.

I never beat you before.

With them last bars from Slade fading out that masterpiece you heard a hundred times before and Stewpot coming in saying good morning again to his multi-million classroom. And Haydn the happiest bum in Pontypridd. Telling you on the way out

Your name came up.

You was mentioned.

What?

In that row.

She shouted your name.

A couple of times.

Sounded like Ben.

Did it?

Then he hit hell out of her.

And she clawed his face.

And he chucked her downstairs.

[8]

And for a while that market takes the lonely from your gut. For in that place there are thousands. There is no rain yet though the clouds are dark and full. Weaving slowly through the pale teeming heaving mass running this bet with yourself that it will drizzle within the hour. Making them grey tarpaulins seep and drip coldly into the drawn faces down the musty necks of that hopeless spendthrift valleys crowd. Deadening their lilting chatter same as fowl in an aviary when nightfall comes. Causing a change from now. Making old women slip and slide and fall heavy on the cobblestones around the stalls. Making gasping men drop their booze-damp pounds into a hundred murky puddles trod in and splashed by a hundred murky kids. Making mouths swear and curse and damn your eyes. Making every soul survive harder even against the will sometimes. For it is never welcome here. The rain. Not on Wednesdays. Never on Saturday.

Passing the handbag stall where Eva Shaw is sitting dyed drinking Captain Morgan neat to keep out the cold and the past. Letting one-eyed Ivor do the selling until the first horse runs at Haydock. Watching eager hands thrusting notes into his coke-shovel palms. And snatching up bargain plastic vinyl handbags before the handles fall off in the excitement.

You got no change coming missus.

Only the change of life.

You give me two pounds exact.

I never saw no bloody fiver.

You got no change coming.

Go tell the police then.

I can tell them same as you.

Piss off.

Seeing him wrap Eva's trash in pink tissue five times over in two minutes flat. And seeing her smile at her rum.

On through that murmuring squeeze past the ribbon stall where you first put eyes on Rachel doing this Saturday hobble for a schoolgirl friend who ran away to Walsall with a Paki in the middle of O levels. And staring at the ginger girl there now and wondering if she was the one.

Quality ribbons mister.

Wrap your Christmas stuff.

All prices up to a pound.

Seeing her fidget through them festoons hanging all around gay and bright-coloured like she is some kind of princess shopping in a Persian bazaar. Except she is ugly. And she don't have no princess face as ever you saw drawn in childish storybooks same as the ones you read out to Miriam now and again when she looks like she understands. Being lies all lies in the back of your mind with Miriam not knowing one bloody thing not to mention she is your creation.

Quality ribbons mister.

Tie your hair up on bath night.

Blue for a boy.

And her ugly face smiling at you from behind the strips of ribbon. Making her look special in that setting like she got no right to be. Same as it was with Rachel. Except you definitely do not think of ugly when you speak her name. And you don't remember Persia when you see her cheeky face.

Three yards of scarlet?

Three yards you said?

Why you want three yards?

You hanging yourself?

     I'm making a flag.

That's nice.

I always wanted a flag.

You can't beat a flag.

Nothing like a good flag.

Remembering her cow eyes sparkle with fun as she cuts that ribbon. Clocking you knowing. Full of signals. Telling you hard as hell how she likes the look of you never mind who you are or where you come from or whether you might be some kind of sex maniac out searching for an easy grind.

You left school yet?

     Yesterday.

     I'm a failure.

I'm not.

See you at eight.

     Cheeky pig.

     Outside Woolworth's.

     Nine o'clock.

And she is there ten minutes early same as yourself never mind the chucking rain driving everyone else off the face of Taff Street huddled here and there dripping dark in doorways like spies waiting for the next bus out of town. With Rachel wearing white

43

plastic and cloppity heels to make her look taller. To make her look older than sixteen.

What they call you?

I bet it's Derek or Raymond.

I bet it's something daft.

How old are you?

    Eighteen.

I live up Cilfynydd.

I'm seventeen in November.

That's only four months.

And you are standing staring at her lit up in the light from Woolworth's wondering about *Bonnie and Clyde* over at the *County*. Except she got ideas on the Regent disco and you don't give a monkey's.

They got this Scotch jockey.

Ooh I love hearing the Scotch.

He got a sexy voice.

All rough it is.

Where do you work?

    Underground.

    I been training ten months.

My father was underground.

Caught his head in the grinder.

Now he got compo.

Seven thousand.

Blind deaf and dumb.

    Nasty.

Paid for the house.

And in the Regent there is the sound of Marmalade throbbing out *Piece of My Heart* for the sake of a hundred swaying bodies same as you and Rachel. Holding her at the waist so you can feel the roll of her hips turning you on.

What they call you?

I think you are great.

    Ben.

I said it was daft.

I never been with a Ben.

44

It don't sound so bad.

My name is Rachel.

Filling her with vodka and lime like she is a bottomless pit. Keeping her company on every short swallow as that music and them bloody awful flasher lights turn you both into nutcases long before midnight. Slurring out wet passions at each other not fit for human ears. Lost almost to the ceiling in that smoke-choked deafening stir.

You never had to get me pissed.

What for?

Jumping on.

I'm ready Ben.

I been ready all night.

Have you?

Undo my zip then.

Not here you daft bugger.

What do you think I am?

You said you was ready.

Not that cowing ready.

You think I'm common?

Yes.

So she unzips you there in the middle of Louis Armstrong. And she is laughing like a pantomime witch till she falls over on the floor. And this big bloke with a sweating face throws you through the door and down the steps into the gutter. With Rachel still laughing hysterical pointing at the moon.

The rain have stopped.

Why?

You going for a picnic?

Leaning on her just to steady up for a second. Stopping her laughing with this big messy kiss. And the two of you tottering towards the coke hoppers at the back of the Regent. Out of sight and sound away from the common herd still shaking crazy high above your heads. Seeing her throw down that white mac on top of this pile of coke. Seeing her hitch up her dress and pull down her tights without so much as a by your leave.

Get on with it for Christ sake.

45

I'm freezing here.

All right for a man.

    Are you a virgin?

Don't be sick.

I invented the pill.

Get at it.

Being as nice a liberty as you ever took not to mention the quickest. With the two of you up out and away from them hoppers even before that Scotch jock gets to play the anthem. Telling Rachel

I got miners' fortnight coming up.

Week after next.

Me and Ernie Smallman.

Down Trecco Bay.

We booked this caravan.

    I might come.

    Just for one week.

    I got to find a job.

Number fifty-five.

Row X.

    I might.

With the first week feeling like January up by the North bloody Pole if you forget it is the last week in July. Being easy to slip that memory down Trecco any time never mind the month of the year. Going on and off Coney Beach fairground till you think you should have discount. Seeing the water chute so many times you get enjoyment just thinking about giving it a miss. And always Ernie got this thirst starting long before open tap down at the *Buccaneer*. Supping up his (and your) flagons straight after breakfast being sometimes pie and chips left over from the night before warmed up by the Calor stove. Till his guts gives out and they got to take him back to Ponty in a taxi after six days. And on the seventh Rachel comes with her suitcase.

I hope you got some money.

And that ginger girl is staring at you from behind her rainbow strips like you got two noses with both of them needing a wipe. Bringing you forward four years to now. And an ugly face where Rachel used to be.

46

Quality ribbons mister?
Handy for Christmas.
Are you buying?
    Ever had a friend called Rachel?
Trying it on?
Rachel who?
    She used to sell ribbons.
Never heard of her.
Only been here three weeks.
Are you buying?
    Three yards of scarlet.
    I'm making a flag.

[9]

To where the Old Bridge straddles the River Taff. Waiting on that grey stone arch automatic like you got no control over where your legs have a mind to walk. With eleven o'clock coming up and going by half an hour or more. Still seeing you staring down at the never-ending belt rushing past underneath. And the first drops of rain feckless yet on your hair and muzzing up the steely glintings of the river surface so it don't reflect the bankings no more. And just being there on account of that is where you said you would see her. Same as usual on a Saturday when Melody is out shopping. Knowing bloody well as how she will definitely not meet you there today. But just being automatic anyway. Just in case what Haydn told you was all a wicked dream. Like a part of your time is cut out and set separate for her only. Like that part can suffer no intrusions. No matter what. You got to be there. Except today you are there for nothing. You know you will not see her lovely face. Nor touch nor feel the warmth of her dark brown skin. Unless it is in your mind. Being the worst place she could get.

    Get her from your thinking O my lamb.

    It is all a bloody cock-up.

47

I love her Lord.

Then go to her my son.

And learn of new things.

Making you reckon as how sometimes that good Lord is having
you on. Tormenting you forward into big trouble. And him sitting
back up there surrounded by his holies and this host of heavenly
angels singing gospel songs day in day out with golden harps and
prophets wandering about all over the place kneeling now and
again chewing over the odd prayer. Telling the good Lord how
holy he is and what a good saviour old Jesus been. And how they
know he loves them and the rest. All hanging about up there
waiting for eternity. And staring down at you. Waiting to see
what happens. Being all right for them on account of it is your
valuable skin at risk. And at the end of the problem all they got
to do is clap or hiss.

And the rain now stinging harder into your face. Whipped up
by this sudden gusting wind curving from under that stone arch
towards the clouds same as a sickle. Whipping you and cowering
you off the Old Bridge in a splash and a slither and a catching of
breath. Standing on the corner where Taff Street meets Berw
Road. Leaning against the wall of Tabernacle Chapel where that
rain cannot soak your clothes. Blinking at the spray kicked up by
this passing fleet of three-tonners heavy with granite from the
Craig yr Hesg quarries. And startled sudden by the ageing shape
of Mad Ike staring into your eyes.

They said you was looking for me.

Only to tell you Ike.

I saw Ivor isn't it.

What he say?

You and Rachel.

You been going for her.

She's my woman.

Keep away.

Ivor got too much to say.

Too bloody much by half.

He seen you with her.

Down the club isn't it?

48

I took her home.
Nothing in it.
Watch what you say.
    It's all saying.
    You say this.
    Ivor says that.
    Rachel will say something else.
    I'm telling you Ike.
    Keep away from her.
    She's in the family way.

With rain drips dropping off the peak of his ripped ratting hat where the stitching have parted above his nose. And onto that nose same as a tear running down the side where he left just a few grey whiskers over from his morning shave. Seeing him rub away that raindrop irritable with the back of his hand. His eyes never leaving yours not for a second.

I know.
She told me.

Staring at him stupid wondering how the hell Rachel got to telling him a private thing like that. And feeling this empty feeling on a suspicion as how he knew about the baby before you did. Not liking that.

She been worried.
She don't want no baby.
    So what?
Might turn out like the first.
Women worry about it.
She got this dread.
We just talked.
    She can talk to me.
    You got no business Ike.
    A personal matter.
She's a good girl.
I never touched her.
Never once.
    You say.
Wanted to.

She's a fine woman.
I made a try.
Read her wrong.
  Ivor saw you.
  Saw you with her.
I was trying.
I read her wrong.
I respect her.
That's no lie.

And Mad Ike is sounding so genuine you can hardly get your mood worked up all whiskers and black ready for calling him rotten and maybe in a frenzy starting some kind of fight. Starting to lose the words you had in mind. And listening saggy-gutted instead.

She loves you Ben.

You are breaking her heart.

With them words rattling down through your bones trying to find some kind of level. And finding empty space instead. Hanging there echoing same as vibrations from a tight wire. Up and down inside that space. Like you are hollow.

She said that?
  I love him she said.
  We been friendly.
  Down the club.
  Maybe six months.
  We talk a lot.

Making you wonder what the hell Rachel can talk about for six bloody months with the longest conversation you had together being less than six minutes except perhaps in the recovery room out East Glamorgan after Miriam got born. And even then there was plenty of blank spaces ending in some kind of squabble. But you never spoke about love. You never done that.

She is all handicapped.
They should have let her go.
Brain damaged they said.
Must be an experiment.
Keeping her alive.

50

Perhaps she'll come Rachel.
Some of them come.

Not her mister.
Have they shown her to you?
Go have a look.
Bloody hell.
I'm ashamed.
They should have let her go.
They kept her alive.
I said no.
They should have listened.

It's not up to you.
My bloody baby.
I got a say.
I earned the right.
I been thirty-six hours.
You don't know nothing.
I earned the right.
I said no.
I said kill her.

You can't.
Some of them come.
She got no brains.

Takes after us.
We are not clever.

Remembering as how her talk was all mechanical and flat. And as how she kept staring at the open door of that ward. Staring scared like she was afraid they might bring Miriam in. Staring and talking automatic. A drugged talk. A drugged stare. Never staring at you. Being just an object. And a reason for speaking.

I don't mean clever.
She is all handicapped.
It's not the same.
Not backward.
Not stupid.
Not just that.
She got no brain.

51

That's what I mean.
>Everybody got a brain.
You never seen everybody.
You never seen her.
What about the ones you never seen?
A mother knows.
Knows when she's ashamed.
>Don't be ashamed.
It's all right for you.
You are a man.
You never gave birth.
A woman feels ashamed.
>All them pills you took.
>Perhaps it was that.
And the river.
It could have been a lot of things.
That don't matter.
It don't matter how.
It don't matter why.
She's out there now.
Stuck full of tubes like straws.
She's alive and she should be dead.
And fault and how don't enter into it.
She turns me sick.
Just to look at her.
>Is she ugly then?
>You never said she was ugly.
Ugly as sin in a bucket.
She is hideous.
Turns me sick.
Better off dead.
They can take her away.
For all I care.
They can put her in Hensol.
They can find her a name.
And they do. And they call her Miriam. Somebody. One of
them who kept her alive. Somebody. All of them. Not Rachel.

Not you. A girlish name. A good name. It felt better once she had
a name. You got to have a name. Even if you are brain-damaged.
   She knows about your bit of spare.
   She was going to jump under a bus.
   That's what she said at any rate.
      What?
When she found out.
Rachel knows.
She knows about the other woman.
      What other woman?
Your bit of spare.
She smelt her on you.
Six months ago.
Started coming down the club.
About that time.
After she smelt her.
      Smelt her?
      What's all this about smelling?
They smell each other.
Women sniff.
They always have a sniff.
And she smelt her on you.
      Rachel don't sniff.
Must have done.
When you wasn't looking.
That's how she knows.
She was going to jump under a bus.
You are lucky Ben.
      Am I?
She met me.
And we talked.
We been talking ever since.
      So you say.
She don't know her name.
Nothing like that.
Don't know who she is.
Rachel don't care who or how.

She just knows.

She smelt her plenty of times.

Your bit of spare.

With this Wonderloaf transit splashing all up his back from a dirty gutter pool where he is standing staring at you. Like that ice-cold wet on his legs never happened. And you wishing as how all that bloody sniffing had never happened neither. Wishing as how Rachel could have kept her nose out of things so to speak. And thinking as how them women must have an edge on their men seeing as you never once sniffed Ike on her. Never once getting any of his pong rich up your nostrils. Except now.

What bit of spare?

I don't know nothing about no spare.

Just be told Ike.

Shag off away from Rachel.

Making him turn sudden like he came. And he is gone through that blue smoke haze back into the jaws of Ponty. Out from sight amongst them soaking throngs heaving bulky along the pavements. Filling the black bruised belly of that greedy town with nourishing coin and paper. Stuffing it eager down her gaping slavering throat all ravenous. Swallowing more and more till her hunger pangs are soothed and she shuts her gluttonous mouth with a final contented snap. Being half-past six Wednesdays and Saturdays.

[10]

So you give Rachel them three yards of ribbon for tying her Christmas parcels. Clocking round the living-room she have decorated special. Transforming the whole place into that same kind of wonderland you remember from baby days with a real Christmas tree wrapped in glitter fibreglass wool and fairy lights that flash on and off till a bulb goes. Reckoning as how she must have gone a bit funny this year on account of never seeing the room so well done out before. And them trimmings are everywhere. All along the ceiling borders from corner to corner crisscross with red and orange streamers and balloons that rise and fall as the warm air above the gas fire circulates and catches them. Stuck up with Sellotape and fastened with pins so you can hardly see the ceiling tiles. And Merry Christmas spelt with an X above the mantelpiece right across the mirror in cotton-wool and lipstick. And some kind of American cop shooting this bloke on the telly with the sound right down.

They are sending her home Ben.

You got to fetch her Christmas Eve.

There's this letter we had.

Did we?

You got to fetch Miriam.

Just for Christmas.

And Rachel don't seem hardly upset at all. Not like she was last year being hysterical at the end of the matter. With the end of the matter being Miriam stopping inside the hospital and you spending most of Christmas Day over her ward staring at her and staring out at the never-ending rain. Messing with them woolly toys and plastic boats you bought her and a dozen other playful items given by the Friends of Hensol. And meeting Melody on the sly at six in Talbot Green and going off with her to them old airfield sheds at the far end of Cowbridge till gone eleven.

You do love me don't you Ben?

Say you love me.

Keep telling me O please.

I love you Melody.

I love you to death.

O don't say death.

I do.

I know.

I do too.

O I want you.

What can we do?

Nothing.

We just got to work it out.

I want you all the time.
But I can't leave Rachel.
I don't have the guts.
I could leave Lew.
Sometimes I think I could.
But there's Glyn.
I got to have my son.
I would have to take him.
I couldn't stand that.
It's stealing.
And I don't want your boy.
I know.
We just got to bear it.
Too much agony.
Everybody gets agony.
That's a sin.
Love is a sin?
Just our kind.
Let me kiss you.

And her loveliness that festive night is a thing you will remember for ever there in this long-forgotten airfield shed where young buck pilots once slept between raids on a far country. Where they dreamed dreams of sweethearts pinned up box-shot Kodaks and scoffed ham and eggs from service-buckled mess tins as them Lancasters you seen on telly and gun turrets and Spitfires and Mosquitoes revved angry outside on the asphalt runways radiating same as spokes from a spindle. From that airfield shed into the distance. Into the night. And the last action just a jumbled memory years before the day you got born.

O make me wait Ben.
Not so soon.
I want it to last.
O please love.
Not like a collier.
Not like a randy bull.
Gentle then.
Very slow.

Sleepy slow.
All loving.
I love you.
    I love you.
O no Ben.
O no.
Christ almighty.
O now now now.
Christ almighty.
O bugger.
O you swine.
O now.
Now.
    Yes.

With this American cop hitting hell out of some kind of half-caste kid actor who breaks loose and runs up this alley where they got this load of police officers waiting with lights and sirens and shotguns.

Is that all right then?

Last year you never wanted Miriam.

We had the same letter last year.

    That was last year.

    I want her home for Christmas.

    Can she walk Ben?

No.

Seeing her tie up four parcels neat wrapped with that ribbon. Watching them slender white fingers give finishing feminine touches to the big bows. Creasing here and there for stiffness. Making the parcels look too good to open. Seeing her fix small labels to each one all methodical. Pushing them in a line to one side so she can see the television screen across the table.

What you been buying then?

    Just a few things.

    I posted the cards yesterday.

    These are for hand-delivering.

    Can you do that?

Who for?

Only local.

A few friends.

That one's for your brother.

He never sent us nothing.

His wife sent a card.

Did she?

Just small things.

For him and her and the kid.

Never came to three pound.

No?

Felt I should.

He's your brother.

He got no one else.

Nor her.

See?

It's Christmas.

Looking at the labels on them parcels. To Ieuan Wyn in Mountain Ash. To Jean and Brian Parry and family in Cilfynydd. To Susan Reynolds in Aberdare. To Mike and Yvonne Forrest in Creigau. And the one for Lew. Giving you the willies when you touch that label. Like there is some kind of time bomb wrapped inside. Tick tock.

I bought them a clock.

Did you?

I'll take it over in the morning.

I'll do that.

You don't have to come.

Say I'm pregnant.

That's no lie.

Hearing just faint that American cop telling how he found out something or other. Being aware that Rachel just gave a little sigh. And clocking her hard wondering if she could ever jump under a bus same as Ike said. And wondering if she still does her sniffing around.

I been thinking about an abortion.

There's abortions these days.

Not like when I had Miriam.

58

I could have an abortion.
        What for?
I got sad feelings.
I don't want another Miriam.
It might happen again.
        It might not.
        You can't say.
What if it is?
I got sad feelings.
All the bloody time.
I could have an abortion.
        Is that what you want?
I don't know what I want.
Except you Ben.
I know I want you.
        You got me.
I just get sad feelings.
Do you love me?
        What do you mean?
        You got a baby going again.
        That's twice.
Do you want me?
        I married you.
        What's all this about wanting?
        What's all this about loving?
        You are my wife.
You never said you love me.
Never bloody once.
        What's saying got to do with it?
        Anybody can say anything.
        You just want to hear words.
        And words are just sounds.
        Anybody can make sounds.
        Even animals.

Except maybe some sounds are real. They can be real even for
you. Even for her. Like the sound of crying. Like the sound of a
low sad sob muffled against pillows in the early hours. Or the

sound of laughing. Real noise without words. Real sounds from out of the soul when there is sadness. When there is joy. Or the sound of the first cry of life. And the sound of the last gasp of death. Telling no lies. Them sounds know what they mean. There is no half truth. No messing about with syllables. No thinking to get it just right. No exactness. Crying and laughing is like that. And there are no words.

I can make sounds.

I can say I love you.

I love you Ben.

God help what I am saying.

I love you.

Hearing music from the telly box. Seeing the credits come up quick at the end of the show stuck trapped in the corner of the room amongst Rachel's paper decorations. And her with that low sad sob muffled behind the sound of her words. And perhaps a tear if you could look.

I love you Ben.

Dying to a whisper locked shameful behind her hands covering the darkness of her face (seeing that much reflected in the screen). Turning your guts like a mixer is at work down there. Churning inside and mashing up your brains till you ooze a kind of pity for her and for you and for what Ike said. Knowing you been told no lies. Not with a sound like that. Letting words fall difficult away from your mouth. Nearly a mumble. Nearly a gasp. Never before said sounds not to her. And sounds you hardly got the right to make. Except she wants to hear them. Except they just come. Bubbling up quiet out of mysterious corners. Till they gather together fighting for self-respect.

I love you too.

[11]

Walking down from Cilfynydd into Pontypridd holding that Christmas-wrapped parcel under your arm same as a Sunday bible. Same as them who pass you (being few and far between) on the way to chapel by eleven and the fidgets by half-past. Dressed for God in black and navy blue and dark grey. And the scent of mothballs strong on the furs of freemasonic wives proud demanding to be noticed by the heathen cleaning their hire-purchased Cortinas in sin-besotted oblivion and wax shampoo.

And the fanaticals with zippered testaments or thumb-worn epistles swinging at their hips from out of the mouth of Paul. Hurrying at a crazy half trot towards Elim and a pentecostal trance till dinner time. Wallowing in the blood of the Lamb and waiting on prayer all eager for speaking in tongues or having a fit.

Had a joyous time last Sunday.

The spirit moved amongst us.

 Get on?

I spoke in tongues I did.

I was all tongues.

I was speaking to the Lord.

 What did you say?

I don't know.

And the Salvation Army marching in columns of one by himself through Ynysangharad Park towards Treforest and the Citadel where God puts him on a charge if he is caught backsliding. Marching stiff severe snappy to the beat of some distant band. Drilled into prayerfulness and military respect beneath the cross of Calvary where Jesus died by numbers.

And the next.

Wheel him in sergeant.

 Left right.

 Permission to speak sir?

 Private Protheroe sir.

61

Left right.

Reporting sick.

Stand up straight man.

So God can see you.

Where's the pain?

In the heart sir.

Somewhere in that region.

Drop your trousers.

Cough twice.

And hold your breath.

Will I make it sir?

Do not abandon hope.

You got sinbosis Protheroe.

Very nasty.

You are just in time.

Is sinbosis curable sir?

Can God help me?

Can he fix me up?

You come to the right place.

God will make you whole again.

Drink this cup Protheroe.

Drink ye all of it.

Mercy mercy.

Thank you.

What was that stuff?

Blood of the Lamb.

You got to sign for it.

I will.

I will.

Arise take up thy bed and so on.

Left right Protheroe.

And the next.

Making you wonder if they got a Salvation Air Force hid somewhere lying in wait ready for the last days you heard about when you was a whelp in Sunday school. Not to mention some kind of Salvation Navy with a commando battalion aboard sneaking ashore in the small hours soot-faced and edgy holding Sankey hymn books between their holy teeth. And surrounding the *Pig and Bedpan* before them illicit boozers can run for an illicit leak. And slipping into action at the drop of a commandment with a whoop and a yell for Jesus. Hitting the *Pig and Bedpan* for six or seven. Lashing into submission every blasphemous soak in sight with a battery of war cries and a bombardment of well-aimed psalms straight (and narrow) from Zion. And mister I can tell you for nothing as how when the last days come around them Salvationists definitely will not be taking prisoners.

Crossing the Merlin Bridge into Pwllgwaun past the *Merlin Inn*, where it have been open tap for half an hour judging by that left-over laughter coming weak through her open doors still giggly from the night before if ever them doors was shut. Into Lee Street where your brother lives. And the rain begins to fall.

Staring down the short length of terraced houses grey-stoned and purple-roofed in the manner of the back of beyond. With beyond being Dan's muck hole poking up still above the tip at the end of the street where kids are playing slides on pieces of tin sheeting even as you did once. And seeing this one black-bummed urchin slide towards you leaving his sheet in an agile leap right at the finish of that run. Letting his momentum carry him along the pavement to where you are stood.

Is that a present mister?
> Yes.
That's my house.
You want Number Eight?
> Yes.
That's my house.
Are you my uncle?
Are you Ben?
> Glyn is it?
> You must be Lew's boy.
I seen your photo.
> My photo?
Mam got your photo.
She don't know I seen it.
She got a locket.

Never wears the thing.

But I seen your photo inside.

And he is gone quick as he came back to Dan's muck hole getting muckier now on account of the morning rain. Leaving you dead scared about that locket being mystified as to how Melody ever got your photo in the first place. Feeling that with her you don't know the half of it anyway. But ringing the doorbell chimes dry-tongued and hoping hard as hell no one inside can hear.

I brought you a present.

Merry Christmas Lew.

  Merry Christmas be buggered.

  Come in you bastard.

With the first chill of brotherly hate running down your spine as you edge by him up the passage into the living-room where no one have bothered to put up any trimmings. Hearing the front door slam shut and then only your breathing and the crackling of paper in your hand around that clock and trinkets. There is no other sound. So you turn and he is standing there staring at you with his nose all plastered up on one side and a creeping bruise from his forehead to his cheek-bone.

What you done?

You had an accident?

What happened to your nose?

  Fell over.

Must have been a bloody fall.

You fall off a cliff?

  Melody is upstairs.

  She cracked her ankle.

  She'll be down in a minute.

  She fell over too.

  Don't sit down you're not stopping.

I never said I was.

  What the hell is this?

  Open it.

And he throws you that locket Glyn mentioned. And your photo is inside right enough. Being a wedding-day snap took by the *Ponty Observer* man outside Courthouse Street registry three years ago. Staring at your newsprint chops smiling back and catching just the corner of Rachel's hat where the picture been cut.

That's my photo.

I know it is.

What the hell is it doing there?

Why have Melody got your photo?

Your wife don't have bloody mine.

Is that right Ben?

And you definitely got to nod to that one. Seeing his face getting all worked up ugly and knowing there is violence in the air. Feeling them familiar waves coming electric out from where he is standing. Covering you same as some kind of thin film invisible but real. Like his words are radio-active.

Why she got your photo?

What do Melody say?

Fuck her.

What do you say?

We been friendly.

Friendly?

What's all this about friendly?

I never heard about friendly.

Not a man and a woman.

What you been doing?

I love her.

Knickers.

You been shagging her.

What's all this about love?

You hardly know her.

Don't tell me answers like that.

Hearing this clump clump on the stairs. Seeing him turn towards the passage where Melody is leaning heavy against the wall swollen-eyed and holding her side like she got a rupture. And there is plaster on her ankle. And mister I can tell you for nothing as how the whole scene is some kind of waking nightmare you want to run away from. Except the sight of her and them radio-active words have sapped your strength for certain. Seeing Lew point at you and through you. Feeling like a target stretched on wires.

He said he loves you.

I love her he said.

More than you bloody said.

You never said that for years.

He don't know nothing.

What do he know?

He's only a kid.

Have he had your drawers down?

It wasn't like that.

Nothing dirty Lew.

It was love.

You hear what he said?

I'm not ashamed.

It was love.

And he hits her off her feet with one thump in the mouth. Hearing her scream just this short scream falling backwards against the other passage wall. And the smack of her bottom hitting the oilcloth. Falling nasty against the gas meter. Hiding her face with her arms.

And this grotty numbness behind your ears humming weak around inside your head at the sight of Melody hit pathetic from standing on her own two legs. Feeling no matter what you got to make a try. So you hold that Christmas parcel tight and you slam Lew in the back of the head. Being not heavy enough nor hard enough for such a definite job. With him lunging forward just one step like all you done was push him a bit. Except that clock is broke and them trinkets spill between your fingers from the wrappings to the floor. Seeing him turn away from Melody to look at you standing there same as some kind of dick gone spastic.

What you done boy?

I hit you.

With that?

What is it?

A present.

Jesus Christ.

66

You hit me with a present?
A bloody Christmas present?
Yes.
You was beating Melody.
She's my wife.
Fuck all to do with you.
I love her.
Jesus Christ.
And he is staring at you like it is all a dream. And you are staring back the same. With this quiet whimpering coming from the gas meter where Melody is still crouched huddled like a broken doll. Seeing him blink in a daze reaching for his parka hung on a chair by the door. And walk drag-footed past her up the passage out into the street. And is gone.
Let me look at you.
I must be a sight.
Why did you come?
There was no need.
And she is a sight all right with this round blood drip welled up on her bottom lip from where her teeth must have bit when she got thumped. Helping her upright and holding her close in the dark of that passageway. Letting her bruised body fall gentle against yours. Holding her long till the last shivers die away.
What happened?
Haydn told me about the fight.
Is your foot broke?
Just a small bone.
Fell from the stairs.
He found my locket.
Glyn showed it to him.
Bloody kid.
I never knew about no locket.
That was pretty stupid Melody.
Something to hang on to.
Feel you near.
Kept it hid.
Thought so anyway.

67

I brought a present.

Just an excuse.

Wipe your eyes.

You been crying a lot?

> Since Friday night.
>
> When he found out.
>
> It's his pride more than anything.
>
> No other feelings.
>
> Just pride.
>
> Don't worry about me.
>
> I can take a knocking.
>
> It's over now.

What do you mean over?

> Him and me.
>
> It's over.
>
> I've had enough.

What do you mean?

> I'm leaving this place.

When?

> When my leg is better.
>
> When I can get about.
>
> When I can run.

Reckoning what she have said to be only angry talk at the end of the matter with her having nowhere to go on this fat earth except where she is right now. Being not much to brag about but enough to make do when you are miles off that first million in the bank. And a long way away from hating every living soul who breathes the air around you. Like sadness is a lingering thing set quite apart from hate. Apart from running. Apart from revenge. Apart from everything and everyone. Except yourself. A good long look inwards. That's sadness. The reason why Melody will not leave Lew. The reason why you will not leave Rachel. Sadness. And you all have your share. It would be easier if there was hate. A blind wilful frenzy of lasting hate. The hate that wants to kill. Wants to destroy. Cannot help despising with every waking second. With every waking minute and hour and day. A festering lust and urge to damage beyond repair. A long way from Melody.

A long way from you. All you got is a gland going pop. All you got is loving. All you got is sadness.

Don't say that.

He don't want you to run.

You got nowhere to go.

I love you.

    I will run.

    I sniffed scent on his pullover.

Not mine Ben.

    I will run.

    I can't stand that.

    I love you too.

He never left you.

Not for her.

Not for the one with scent.

He never done that.

And she is crying again huddled into you. Feeling for the back of your neck with her fingers and reaching your lips with her own. Till you kiss and squeeze and feel the warmth rise out of her lovely body in an ecstasy of contact against your own.

We could run together.

We could run now.

It don't matter where.

    Rachel got a lump.

    She's in the club.

    You got to know that.

You said she can't.

She's on the pill you said.

    We been distant for nearly a year.

    She stopped taking the bloody things.

    And we got together once or twice.

    Just lately.

    You'd never think.

    She's carrying all right.

And she don't say nothing more. And she stops her crying. Just wanting to be held close. Being like that old universe have descended all around the both of you at last. Gulping you down

helpless till the only thing left to do is stand there waiting to be
forgotten by every eye that ever saw you. By every hand that ever
touched your flesh. By every mind that ever shared your thinking.
Telling her funny-throated

I got to go now Melody.

I'm working tonight.

You take care my love.

And she nods turning to limp away into the living-room out
from your sight. And you walk back up Lee Street with the sound
of them urchins shouting faint as they slide the day away happy
on that muck heap where dreams are made beautiful and old men
shiver in the wind.

[12]

And underground that night you breathe a lot of dust same as
the rest of Beano's gang. Setting up this new seam facing for the
firemen who don't like cutting their hands. Hacking and picking
all manual till the small hours. Burrowing in deep through them
Maritime vaults. Shifting skiff after skiff of hardcore rubble.
Making you think as how you have drawn your last load of bitu-
men in that district. Cursing the surveyors up in heaps for saying
there will be coal after eight to eleven feet. And still hacking rock
after fourteen.

With a lot of coughing and spitting for hours there in the dark-
brown gloom slashed occasionally through the dust by lamp
beams and voices desperate for air.

They sent us the wrong bloody way.

There's no coal in this end.

Surveyor must be pissed.

He got his instrument twisted.

Thinks he's bloody chocolate.

Send the bastard down here.

Put a pick up his hole.

Bloody office boys.

70

But finding coal after fifteen feet running Vee pattern. And a seam they can blow out continuous for six months or more. Crawling back on your bellies to the last deadface where the gang sit down coughing in chorus. And mister I can tell you for nothing as how around this town they call that noise the national anthem.

Remembering Tommy and the way he went off to meet his maker two years past with lungs full of pneumoconiosis and blind in both eyes and deaf in both ears and a tongue that couldn't talk on account of all them wires holding his jaw together. Being Rachel's old man who fell into the grinder sorting good coal out from bad. Fed on baby food through plastic tubes. Looking like a Martian dribbling glucose from his agonised gob. And only then in between long sucks of oxygen up his nose behind this ugly green face bag you finally use when you got over ninety per cent inside them dust-filled organs.

Hearing still Rachel telling him the last words she would ever speak to his muted mangled face. And him not knowing she was in the room till she gives him a kiss on one of them blind eyes.

Ben have come to sit with you.

He have come for company.

That's a full cylinder.

You are OK now Dad.

The doctor says not to worry.

I'll give you a wipe.

There's like a baby you are.

You are OK now Dad.

Mam have gone to Ponty.

Ben have come to sit with you.

Staring at the poor bastard who never heard nothing of what she said. Staring at him. Sightless milky white eyes fixed on the ceiling. Gasping out his last. Creamy grey-faced up and down horribly in rhythm with his chest. Thin as a starved herring. A fading shadow of the man he once was judging by his photo on the dresser standing smiling fat twenty years ago outside Coney Beach fairground arm in arm with his collier opos on a sunny day.

Hearing the hiss from the cylinder valve now and then as he regulates his breath. And the smell of camphor strong on his Daz-white pillow-case. And he have never seen you. And you have never bought him a pint down the club nor anywhere. Yet in the loneliness of the fag-end of his life his hand reaches out for yours like something have told him you are there.

And his thin fingers grope across yours and he feels your nails and he feels your palm and he grips your thumb. And through all them jaw rivets and silver wires his lips part into something of a smile. Giving you the willies for certain on account of you knowing he is definitely not smiling because he is happy but because his fingers have told him you work down the pit.

And mister I can tell you for nothing as how you don't ever forget that smile. Like he is showing you the end of your life. And how you had better look hard while you still got eyes.

Except you are not stupid like he been. And they will never catch you near no grinder after your coal-pulling strength have gone. And the bastards will never shelve you off to woman's work same as they done to poor Tommy. Look what happened to him once he lost his self-respect.

Telling them deaf ears as how they will never keep you there underground as long as him. Just long enough to pay off the house and throw away that rope from around your neck. Just long enough to work a bit of safe compo same as plenty you know. Not like him. Never like that.

And all the while you are telling him he is holding your hand. And that beginning of a smile don't ever leave his broken mouth. Letting him stop like that for an hour or more till his fingers get cold and your arm grows numb.

Staring at his photo outside the fairground and wondering if it was at the end of miners' fortnight or at the beginning. And remembering how you stood in that selfsame spot alongside the helter-skelter waiting for Rachel to slide down on her mat five times before she was sick.

Calling her rotten for pushing her luck after three pints over in the *Jolly Sailor* where you had to lie about her age. And lifting her up off the floor outside the *Golden Goose* when she fell down pissed out of her mind. Telling her just for the fun of seeing her colour go from cream to white.

What you need is a bag of chips.

And pretending to take her inside that Wimpy bar where the stink of grease was enough to paralyse a horse.

I want to go home.

I want to go home.

Holding her tight so she don't fall again past the *Buccaneer* where the singing is great. Past Jack Williams' betting office. Round the back of the Model Village where them gnomes is kipping fast. And through the miniature golf area running on to the car park where you both have this jimmy riddle behind some clapped-out Consul.

I got a pain Ben.

I want to go home.

>You can't go home.

>Only today you come.

Did I?

Is this Porthcawl?

>Yes.

>We got a caravan.

Letting her lean heavy against you crossing the car park and up through the municipal site onto Trecco where this matchbox kingdom begins and ends as far as the eye can see. So many square miles of trailers. Row upon row between sand and gravel. Set in some kind of pattern only a bird could understand. Or a collier when he needs his bunk.

Trecco Bay owned and ruled over invisible by W. R. Thomas and Sons just after the last war when there was only two trailers. With them trailers being male and female encouraged to breed by old W.R. till you see what you can see tucked there on the elbow of Porthcawl. A caravan world. A paradise of booze and betting. With discotheques for the kids and bingo for the women. With sand and grit blown wild by that south-west wind to help you remember not to forget as how the sea is round the corner waiting hungry for the brave and merciless for the simple.

73

Trecco Bay where they got sand and trailers enough to start another world. And they got the Trecco Restaurant and the Post Office and the Delicatessen and Happy Snaps and Fulgoni's and the Superstore and Cook 'N Take and Cinema 2 and the *Showboat Bar* and the *Bavaria Bar* and the *Merrie England* tavern and the *Dirty Duck* and Jack Malvisi for an honest bet. And they got a church. And they got Caesar's Palace.

And they got row X. And they got a caravan numbered fifty-five.

I can't see out of my eyes.

O Ben put me to bed.

> You got to sleep it off.
>
> You been drinking too quick.

You said be quick.

That's what you told me.

> Not that bloody quick.
>
> It have hit you for six.
>
> We was going for a swim.

Was we?

What for?

> We agreed.
>
> Not now.
>
> You are pissed.

I can't swim.

I never said that.

> I was going to teach you.
>
> Tonight.
>
> A midnight swim.

Waves frighten me.

I hate the sea.

If you can call that boiling grey mess of pollution a sea. Being just the Bristol Channel at the end of the matter running on down from out of the Severn River and changing gradual into nothing special except where it sicks up over them red-flagged rocks around Trecco and Coney Beach leaving what it swallowed from the night before strung out stinking across them cut-knuckled acres same as a bog that never got flushed.

74

Plenty of seaweed and splinters of wood worn smooth by the undercurrents. Oil-stained plastic bags. Two dead gulls clogged to death by tar and Shell-Mex. Left half of a brassiere worn to ruin before that final fateful stretch. French letters (three) and a dogfish all in the same green pool. One Woodpecker bottle (empty) leaning upside down. Doll's head (negroid). Doll's body (caucasian). Chipped forty-five record with the label gone. Pages fifteen to forty-six of *One Day in the Life of Ivan Denisovich* (you read it after Solzhenitsyn got slung out of the Soviets). And Rachel.

What you doing down here?

What you leave me for?

I been looking everywhere.

> You was sleeping.
>
> Looked like you needed it.
>
> I come for a walk.

This place stinks.

Come back to the trailer.

Please Ben.

I got a chill through me.

> Beer shivers.
>
> It's not cold.

Got a fag?

> No.

I got to get some.

Where's the money?

And there's nothing to eat.

> There's chip shops all over.

I don't want bloody chips.

Not after last night.

I want Sugar Puffs.

I always have Sugar Puffs.

And there's no tea.

You got bugger all.

Give me some money.

Watching her scrabble back awkward across the rocks holding this five pound note for buying herself together again. And she does. And she is cheap at the price. And bloody good value for the time of year.

His daughter. Tommy's legacy to the world. A little bit of him. And him lying there with them cold fingers clenching your hand like he knows you been staring at his photo. Like he knows now as how he is a mockery of his former self and the end product of nothing much at all.

Except poor Tommy is dead. And he don't know one bloody thing no more.

Pulling his fingers off your hand with the raging willies up and down your skin bringing on the shivers. Listening for his breathing to start up again. But it don't. Giving him a shake or two just to get the clockwork whirring. But it don't whirr and the shaking makes him go lop-sided in that camphor-stunk bed.

Remembering the smile wiped off his busted chops as he lies there dead and white and cold-looking. Seeming smaller than ever you have known him to be small. And turning off the cylinders so the gas don't go to waste in a boxed tight lung.

And shouting down the stairs for Rachel a couple of times on account of her pegging out clothes up the back. And her running pathetic into the bedroom. And taking one look at Tommy before she runs out again to the noise of this bloody awful gazooker jazz band blowing and thumping snare drums outside passing in the street below. Like the village have come out special to help him quicker into heaven or wherever it is that colliers go.

With Beano poking his fingers into your side and offering this plug of twist he just broke off from a fresh screw. With the coughing dropping to the odd whimper now and just this jaw munching slorrip from end to end along that line telling you as how it have been a hard dig that night and who knows maybe a year off the life of every chewing gob.

That'll fix the bastards.

That'll trim their wicks.

Chew it Ben.

I owe you a knob.

Did Tommy work with you?

Was he ever here Beano?

Caught his head in the grinder.
    I know.
Had his own gang.
Bottom district.
Nothing to do with me.
Before my time.
Nobody remembers.
    I do.

[13]

So you fetch Miriam home the day before Christmas. And she is sitting there on the settee staring only at this big white bear Rachel bought off the market. And no amount of talking from you nor from Rachel can make her take her eyes off that furry thing. Like it is the only toy she ever saw. And all she wants to know about.

She don't say much Ben.
Don't she ever say much?
    She don't say nothing ever.
    She can only make noise.
    I told you plenty of times.
I thought she might say something.
She never made a sound yet.
    You got to stroke her.
    You got to be gentle.
    Have you kissed her?
No.
    You should kiss her Rachel.
    Show her it's all right.
    She knows about kissing.
And watching Rachel stoop over Miriam to kiss her on the cheek so the child gets startled and fluttery with them thin disjointed arms.
    She hit me.

77

She knocked me on the nose.
She flung her hand in my face.

> You scared her.
> She's easy to scare.

It never hurt Ben.
She never tried to hurt.
A mother can tell.

> You got to watch it.
> That's all Rachel.
> You got to watch it.
> Creeping up on her.

I never crept.
I'm her mother.

> She don't know that.
> Not yet.

Not yet?

> Bound to take time.
> Give her time.
> Kiss her again.
> Kiss her hand.

And she does. And Miriam don't flutter no more. But she
stretches out them arms towards you like she does down Hensol
sometimes. Telling you for certain though she don't talk nor use
words as how she wants picking up and caressing same as any
other young animal who is scared of new sounds and new smells
and the feel of different skin.

Can I hold her Ben?

> Sometimes she wriggles.
> You got to hold tight.

Seeing Rachel hold her close for nursing. And swaying backwards and forwards to some rhythm she got going inside her head.
With Miriam liking all that kind of fuss and nestling her face
into Rachel's neck.

She's licking me Ben.
I can feel her tongue.

> She got a tongue all right.

It's like a love bite.

78

Perhaps she's doing that.

Till Rachel gets the hang of nursing that child. Kissing her now and then same as some kind of long-lost mother-woman with this great load of catching up to do. Till Miriam falls fast asleep in her arms. And in a whisper Rachel smiles her mouth away.

I got her bed ready.

The cot's in our room.

I'll take her up.

You go out for a drink.

I got plenty to do.

The turkey have thawed.

You go out Ben.

I'll be all right.

So you take off in the car down the *New Inn* where this Chamber of Trade bunch got a party going upstairs. And knowing as how their laughing and screaming is definitely not for the likes of you. Slipping down to the basement bar where the booze is cheaper and where Gwen Ann pulls you a pint of Whitbread.

That's for nothing Ben.

Got left behind the bar.

Who from?

Beano and some men.

They was in earlier.

Beano owes me.

Tell him thanks.

With the basement bar only half full considering it have gone nine. Reckoning as how all that bow tie and frills upstairs wandering here and there supping shorts is upsetting for a lot of regulars who only ever saw Tories dress like that. Reckoning as how the sight of any Conservative invasion through Ponty is enough to turn a clear pint cloudy and make a double vodka taste like turps.

That pint was off.

You bloody drank it.

I was thirsty.

I'm just saying.

Just voicing an opinion.

Have another?

79

Yes.

Have one yourself Gwen Ann.

You could do with filling out.

Clocking them beautiful fingers curl around that draught handle and pull gentle towards her breasts taut under her black sleeveless polo-neck like she is drawing a line. Biting out that first mouthy gulp and wiping this white froth mark away with her tongue. And staring sparkle-eyed at you reflected from the pink strip neon framing her spirits rack.

Lew came in last night.

Him and his cronies.

Billy had to take him home.

Pissed out of his mind.

    Is that right?

And that woman was with them.

The one from the market.

Takes a room here sometimes.

    Eva Shaw.

He was calling you rotten.

    We don't get on.

Said you been messing.

    Messing?

With his wife.

Messing about.

Called you all kinds of four letters.

He got it in for you.

    We have never got on.

He hates your guts.

I don't call that not getting on.

I call that real nasty Ben.

What you been doing?

    Nothing.

Funny kind of nothing.

She have left him.

    What?

He said anyway.

She took off yesterday morning.

Took their kid.

>I never knew that.
>What did he say?
>Where have she gone?

He never said.

Just called you rotten.

Giving you a pain deep inside the gut so bad that Gwen Ann's face begins to shimmer like a mirage and her voice comes over you in loud and quiet waves so that nothing is distinct no more. Nothing except this vision of Melody out there somewhere with Glyn. And somewhere being God knows where. With Christmas in the morning.

She broke her ankle.

>They said.

Who said?

>Lew's cronies.
>They was having a good laugh.
>Not him though.
>It was serious to him.
>You could tell that.
>Well you don't have to tell do you?

No.

>He thinks she have gone with you.
>They said she never.
>They told him that.
>Billy saw her on Ponty station.
>Her and the kid.

Billy?

>He collects the *Western Mail*.
>Early morning.
>Off the Cardiff train.
>Saw her and the kid.

Where was they going Gwen Ann?

>I don't bloody know.
>Could be anywhere.
>What you done to her?

Nothing.

81

That's the trouble.
Men don't know nothing.
Not what a woman feels.
Not deep inside.
I been through it.
Never again.
Men are not worth it.
Want another pint?
Double Bell's.
You have one Gwen Ann.
If ever I come back after I die.
I want to be a bloody man.

Seeing her pour this double tot into the bottom half of her pint
but filling the tot glass again and shoving it between your elbow
and your beer. And letting her take a pound from the top pocket
of your jacket like she thinks you are no longer capable of thinking
straight or something. Being just about right in any man's lan-
guage. With all that talk about Melody upping and leaving Lew
having knocked you for six never mind about him running
around telling all the wide world.

Be sure your sins will find you out.
You got your hands full mister.
Serves you bloody right.
We had plans.
Me and Melody.
She's a black isn't it?
I heard she was black.
I never seen her.
Dark brown more than black.
Only black when the light have gone.
Fell for her did you?
All the way was it?
Yes.
Gwen Ann you got too much mouth.
It was all the way.
Can't have been.
What do you mean?

82

She's out there.
You are in here.
Can't have been.
Not all the way.
     It would have been.
They all say that.
I'm telling you.
Men don't know nothing.
Not how a woman feels inside.
Our insides are different.
You know that?
You ever thought about it?
Stands to reason.
Our insides is not the same.
But we never learn.
None of us ever learn.
I've said I'm finished with men.
But I'm not.
It's a lesson we can't ever learn.
We are born to be simple.

And she swills off her beer and double whisky in one long swallow. Leaving you for a while on account of this pair of Tories who have crept down from the party in search of Whitbread. And you notice as how they look at you and Gwen Ann same as a dog man might look at a cat. Except you are in no mood to get funny with the likes of them. Turning away from the bar to find a dark corner where you just don't have to talk.

Not being positive in your mind as to whether you might go after Melody even if you knew where to follow. But being positive that you should. And that conflict turning from empty shame into whiskers and black staring dimly up at you on the surface of that tot.

You have learned of new things O my lamb.
Love is guts ache.
     And a bit of fun.
You had your bit of fun my lamb.
Now you got the guts ache.

There is more guts ache than fun.

    Too bloody royal Lord.

    I wish I knew where she was.

She have gone O my lamb.

    Will she come back?

I expect so.

They usually do.

Women don't learn eff all.

They are not like men.

I made the buggers simple.

    Gwen Ann said that Lord.

    Them was her words exact.

I am in the mind of all living things.

Nothing is spoke without me knowing.

I am the great I am I am.

That's what I am.

    I cocked up her life O Lord.

    Melody was doing all right.

You stuck your beak in my lamb.

After that she let it grow.

    Did she?

She could have stopped it.

She needed love.

Needed to be loved.

And that good Lord vanishes in a bursting bubble from out of the dark brown depths of your shaking tot. So you drink it off. And Gwen Ann comes across with another double. Looking all informative and helpy the way women do sometimes. Sitting opposite you where she can see the bar quiet for a few minutes.

Whisky's off.

    What you want to do is forget her.

    You got a lovely wife.

    I seen you with her in town.

    What you want to do is forget Lew's woman.

Melody.

I love her.

    Don't you love your wife?

I don't hate her.
Stop interfering Gwen Ann.

    And you got a little girl.

    They said there was a little girl.

Handicapped.
Brain have gone wonky.

    That don't matter.

    There's flesh and blood between you.

    Between you and your wife.

    Flesh and blood.

    The little girl is depending.

    She is depending on you.

    One of God's women.

    We are all God's women.

    We got to be loved.

    We can't be thrown away.

I threw Melody away.
She was depending.
I never had no guts.
Melody had all the guts.
Don't interfere Gwen Ann.

    If you loved her.

    If she felt that.

She did.
All the time.
I still feel it.

    That will be enough for her.

    That will help her to be brave.

    Women are made simple.

    And to be brave.

Seeing off that double in two shivering sips with the taste of it
starting to calm down but muzzing up through the roof of your
mouth into the bottom of them scrabbling brains. Making you
speak braver than that tongue could utter half an hour previous.
Staring at Gwen Ann's finger drawing circles in this fag ash some
filthy bum left on the mahogany.

    If I knew where she was I could go to her.

I wouldn't mind going to her in any case.

No good Ben.

You can't wipe out her feelings.

She is better off on her own.

Her leg was broke.

Lew must have done it.

She said she fell.

I got a feeling.

He been beating her.

He got no cause.

She's his woman.

She been playing around.

He got riled.

Felt small.

I know how it is.

Do you?

My husband threw me out.

It was nine years ago.

You got no ring.

He divorced me.

Did he?

Still feel rotten.

Woman always feels rotten.

It was adultery.

Was it?

They said in court.

Did they?

I called it love.

I loved him.

I still love him.

Who?

My correspondent.

He's married.

Still bloody married.

And you are looking at nine years of adultery with her correspondent drawn across those pinched and suffering chops. Nine years of belonging and nine years of not belonging depending on the time of day or night. And it definitely didn't do much for Gwen Ann in the way of making her beautiful. Starting them haggard lines around her eyes and mouth. Looking fifty though you know she can't be more than thirty-five at the very most. And wondering how Melody might look after nine years of moonlighting never mind yourself. With the wonder being it can last so long in the first place.

Why don't he divorce her?

Why don't he leave her Gwen Ann?

Why don't he play the game?

      He got a mind of his own.

      And he don't want to hurt his wife.

      She knows all about it.

      But she pretends otherwise.

      They just carry on.

I couldn't stand that.

Not nine years.

      Easy said Ben.

      But it just happens.

      And there it is.

      Nine years gone.

      Just like that.

      He'll be in soon.

      It's his time.

You got a pattern.

      We all got a pattern.

      Trouble is breaking it.

      A pattern is hard to break.

      You are lucky.

I don't feel lucky.

      You broke your pattern.

      With Melody.

      You broke it.

      I call that lucky.

      Something positive.

      Now forget her.

      You got to forget.

Keep boozing.
Then go home.
Live a life mister.
Keep boozing.

And you do. And the bar gets fuller nearing half-past ten. With dark shapes nudging and jostling you and calling you Ben though them shapes can never take on a single name. Till Mad Ike brushes past you up to the counter. And Gwen Ann smiles at him. And she strokes his cheek. And calls out time.

[14]

With the first thought you have standing outside the *New Inn* being as how some sod have stole your car. Till you remember where you put it around the back in Market Square. Except you got a job (first off) telling which Avenger is green there being four parked all told in front of the Co-op arcade. And all of them looking orange under the street lighting. Like everything in the world have gone the same colour in some kind of mighty confusion set deliberate for making drunken men go blind in honour of Christmas.

You got no chance mister.

With this hand coming out from nowhere and holding your wrist so them car keys jangle falling on to the cobblestones. Turning short-sighted to stare at his orange face.

If you get in I will test you.

Better off walking isn't it.

　　Who?

Breathalyser.

I got my little bag ready.

Better off walking.

You know a good turn?

And that police officer stoops to pick up your keys. Shoving them inside your pocket and telling you straight

You will lose your licence.

You got no chance mister.

And he definitely don't look more than twenty if he have even reached that great age. Seeing him stand off waiting to see what you will do. Knowing as how if you got any brains in your head you will do like he says. Reckoning to come back down in the morning when he have gone and his little breathing bag with him.

Much obliged officer.

I am a family man isn't it.

You done me a great favour.

The walk will do me good.

And never once do you tell him what a sneaking little phallus-sucking bastard he been. Hiding up the arcade same as a rattle-snake waiting to pounce on any innocent citizen who may have outstayed his welcome (just a bit) in a local tavern. And who happens to have a set of car keys in his hand. And who (on account of his unstinting diligence) have now got to walk home the thick end of two miles with legs like broken bulrushes and a head full of rattling bottle tops.

Thank you again officer.

May the Lord look upon you.

And bless you with his goodness.

That's all right squire.

Now fuck off home.

And in Taff Street everything is jumping up and down as you walk along the centre of the road. Hearing your footsteps hollow-sounding echoing back from the deep-set doorways where many a caress is long under way.

Past Halfords with a half-empty window display sold silly to hundreds of Father Christmases fresh into Ponty from the never never lands of Porth and Ynyshir and Ferndale and the rest. With never never being what it's all about at this time of year.

Passing Cohen's where his window have made a spectacle of itself and where the eyesight testing card is standing upside down on top of these tiny-tot binoculars. And the hanging clock outside twinkles half-past twelve.

So you cross the Old Bridge into Trallwn where they call the

89

streets North West South and East with that main road down the middle called Middle Street to defy the imagination of all who come to live at the sharp end of Pontypridd. And you walk down Middle Street passing a rat on the window-sill of number eighty-six chewing this cabbage stump he have picked out from one of the ash bins rolling gentle in the wind. Walking wide around him in case he got a notion to jump. Hearing this distant ding-a-ling sharp through the wind as a fire engine pelts up the freeway or maybe an ambulance racing down to Cardiff. And stopping standing staring swaying at the angry red glow in the night above Cilfynydd. And thinking it is pretty.

On to the Merthyr road where you lose sight of that glow on account of the houses being so tall. But seeing this fire tender hum past flashing blue lamps same as laser beams seething with energy. Causing you to lean against the wall with the intoxication of it all. And leaning there watching three police cars flash on by after that tender. Wondering who been doing wickedness this early Christmas Day.

With fairy lights flicking on and off in more than one window. And a fibreglass-hung Christmas tree lit beautiful in the bedroom above Pegler's stores.

Feeling pukey by now so you got to look around for a drain to honk over. But leaning instead over this low white garden wall and vomiting into some keen bugger's rose bushes pruned low ready for the Spring. And this front door opening to your left with a short bald bloke standing staring at you mercilessly in your illness.

Filthy rotten sod.

Go and honk in your own garden.

Ought to be made to mop it up.

Merry Christmas.

Filthy rotten pig.

Scum I call you.

Dirty drunken cow.

Scum is what you are.

Moving on quick in case all that baldness is catching. Up King's Hill where that glow bursts across the sky strong and wild.

Where you know it is coming from the top street. And sobering quick as hell on account of that is where you live.

Stumbling awkward in the back-lane darkness behind Ann Street. Falling on the steps hard across your knees so you gasp with the pain. Hearing loud shouts and a bit of screaming in Wood Street even before you round the corner.

And in that street it is so bright you could swear it was day.

Running down Wood Street half tripping over long thick canvas hoses screwed into branch pipes and hydrants. With the stink of smoke racing that pulse into frenzy. And the sight of flames ten foot long shooting out of upstairs and downstairs. Cracking through the air above that shouting screaming crowd. And fizzing and whirring bits from the plaster exploding into the street out of the belly of that inferno gone wild beyond control of mere water. And your face washed in the heat. And your eyes fogged by the smoke. And all of your body rigid with fear. Gaping dumb at the place where you live.

Must be dead Ben.

They are still inside.

What?

[15]

Seeing the hoses pounding water into the house. Through the bedroom windows upstairs and downstairs into the parlour. Through the front door where the smoke belches out like there are tyres burning in the passage. And the crackling and the spitting getting less. And Beano at your elbow strapped up with breathing apparatus stamped NCB.

Can't touch it yet Ben.

They got no chance.

I don't think so.

With the powerful hum of them diesel pumps drowning out his words. And being shoved to one side as a fireman runs a ladder to the bedroom window. But seeing him stand back from the

91

scorching groping flames. And shouting for another hose to be played up there.

Feeling your feet all soggy from standing in that river which is Wood Street. With the bleep and metallic voices talking matter of fact over them police radios. And the cars and the fire engines and the ambulances still flashing urgent blue across the faces of that ugly crowd. Staring gawping gossiping. Better than the telly. This is real. This is free. How nice it feels to feel sorry. How sad. How awful. What a shame. Hair in curlers. Minus teeth. Wearing vests. Wearing pyjamas. Hanging out of windows. Are they dead?

Give me that mask Beano.

I'm going inside.

With the heat from inside that oven meeting you like a blast as you run into the passage. Clawing away the smoke from in front of your eyes shielded by the face mask. Clawing it away and seeing nothing only black. Reaching for the light switch and flicking it up and down. Nothing. And moving along the passage. Feeling your way towards the kitchen. And the heat from the walls making you draw back that hardened palm like you was covered with baby skin. Hearing the popping from the rafters above your head. And opening the kitchen door where there is nothing except smoke and the jet from a hose-pipe bashing against the ceiling showering you and making you gasp.

Into the middle room burnt only on one side in the reflected light from the parlour still an inferno. And the heat in the middle room have blown out the front of the telly so you are treading on broken glass. And clouds of thick smoke billowing from the carpet wherever you tread. And the walls are smoking and charred. And everything have been reduced to a smaller size. Going as near to the parlour as you can get and shouting Rachel and gulping down the smoke till you got to hang your head low near the floor shoving that mask back over your face.

And half-way up the stairs you are passed by this fireman who is pointing for you to get back. But the booze have deadened some of your feelings and you don't suffer hurt like a sober man. Following him onto the landing. And hearing this roar same as a waterfall outside the front bedroom where you sleep. And the fireman points at the door and brings his torch beam steady on to the handle. And you can see the paint bubbling down the wood like a blow-torch been at work. And you give him a nod. Seeing him stare at you from behind his mask all wide-eyed. And you nod again so he knows they will be in there.

Kicking the door open and bowling flat along the landing as the flames gush out over everything. And all in an instant lying there seeing the bed ablaze and a black tump lying stretched in the middle.

And mister I can tell you for nothing as how you don't ever forget that black tump as long as you live. Nor the smouldering from it right through nearly to the bed frame. Blazing all around but dying down as the jets from outside soak that hideous room. Hearing that fireman shouting at you lying on his belly.

Is that the bedroom?

Was they inside?

Yes.

I can see them.

Is that them?

Crawling forward till you reach the bed. And your guts burning painful through the floorboards. With smoke crept inside your face mask so you got to take it off. And the stink of cooked meat. The sickly stink of Rachel and Miriam. And honking uncontrolled all over that black heap. And seeing this little arm poking out from the middle like Rachel lay on top of her baby in some kind of protection. And the hand on that little arm clenched into a fist.

So you touch that smoking heap. You grab at it. And you scream out with the burning. And the roof explodes above your head. There is a thud in your back making you fall sideways. And you bang into something. With that something picking you up and slumping you over his shoulders. And carrying you down into the street where they sit you in the back of this ambulance.

I been in.

There's nothing downstairs.

I know Beano.

I found them.

They are in the bedroom.

Are they gone?

Aye.

And there are faces around that ambulance you never seen before. Gawping faces. Frowning faces. Eager faces. A woman in a nightdress and a policeman wearing a white helmet telling her that you are the husband. That you are all right. Being bloody funny to hear it said seeing as you can only breathe in long gasps and only keep your eyes open for seconds at a time. Till this ambulance man climbs in and shuts the door. Giving you sucks of oxygen (sweet-tasting) from this box contraption resting on a stretcher.

Been in have you?

My wife and kid.

Nasty.

Nasty business.

Wonder how it happened.

Did she smoke?

What?

It was in the bedroom isn't it.

Perhaps she been smoking.

Perhaps.

It don't matter though.

It don't matter how.

No it don't matter how. It don't matter why. And there is no room for if's or maybe's. It is. It is and that's all that matters. They are dead. Facts. Facts for living with. Dead and gone. No more to speak nor run nor laugh nor cry nor smile nor frown. Nor nothing. That's all that matters. And this fat earth is emptier for them sad facts.

You'll have to identify.

I expect you will.

Will I?

Next of kin.

Yes.

And through them dark blue windows you can see two stretchers

94

coming down the steps of your house with the flames now no more than flickers through the open door. Seeing another ambulance back up towards the stretcher bearers. And they vanish from sight.

They got them out then?

    Looks like.

    Take them away now.

    East Glamorgan.

    You don't have to go.

    Not yet at least.

I want to.

    We'll follow them is it?

    Get your hands fixed.

    You can please yourself.

    I'll leave this switched on.

And he goes out shutting the van door again behind him leaving you to lie down on the long blanketed seat staring at the roof light swaying to and fro as you follow Rachel and Miriam out to East Glamorgan mortuary.

I got them safe O my lamb.

They are both up here now.

    Are they still burned up?

    Is Miriam still mental Lord?

I got their souls O my lamb.

Their bodies is buckshee.

You can bury the bodies.

I got no use for skin and bone.

I have taken what I want.

    Merry Christmas Lord.

    Tell them I am sorry.

    Tell them I was coming home.

With Rachel's mother fixing up the funeral arrangements through Ieuan Watts who been preaching the word heavy around this town for a very long time. And him coming out regular from the back streets of Pwllgwaun on Wednesdays and Saturdays with them gold-painted banners he got for scaring the heathen market hordes towards salvation in the name of the Lord.

Reckoning as how that man must have a load of guts to walk through Ponty down the middle of Taff Street yelling shrill as how Jesus saves and as how God is love and as how everybody got to lift their eyes towards Zion same as him. And him not giving a wank for all the mockers who point and snigger superior on account of feeling they are not as loose in the head as he must be. With others telling lying tales about how he likes feeling little girls and little boys with their trousers down behind the tips. And about how he have been knocked down twenty times in Taff Street for walking in the middle. And as how he is cock-eyed if you take away his triple-lens glasses. And as how he gets pissed on brandy every night upstairs in his rat-infested house. And plenty more stories made up to put you off him for good if you got a mind ready for being put off.

Except you don't get put off. And you are glad he is doing the burial never mind his faded burberry and ratting hat. Never mind what the liars have to say behind his stooping back. For you have heard him pray. And you have seen him cry tears for Rachel and Miriam straight from the eyes of heaven.

So the night before the funeral Ieuan Watts comes up to Cilfynydd on his bike where you are stopping with Rachel's mother till the insurance have fixed your house ready (or good enough) for living in again. And he brings his bike into the passage out of the rain with this great crackle of oilskins and leggings dripping over everything same as spray from a waterfall. Clocking him wipe them triple-lens glasses so he can see what he is doing in amongst the wetness of it all. And pulling out this damp rolled-up exercise book from inside the front of his heavy-belted trousers like a conjurer. Being his diary and filing records cum appointment book and order of service prompter at the end of the matter. And the most valuable book he got next to the Bible.

Seeing him sit there steaming on the sofa supping PG Tips with raindrops plopping from the end of his ratting hat into the saucer. And you stare at the bicycle clips on the ragged ends of his trouser legs. And his black boots laced tight with parcel twine. Reckoning as how he must be in his seventies and looking a bit older than when you saw him last a week ago out East Glamorgan Hospital the morning after the night before.

Undertaker have booked in for eleven o'clock.

The two together.

Separate prayers.

A tragic business for you both.

Shall we have a word?

Ask God's blessing on the funeral arrangements.

And he puts down his cup and saucer on the arm of the sofa and kneels on the mat. So even though he don't ask you know as how you got to kneel too on account of him taking off his ratting hat in reverence and holiness. And seeing he is bald with blue scars criss-cross where once his hair grew.

And he prays for guidance to take him through the burial to-morrow even though he have done it a thousand times before.

And bless the boy here Lord.

And bless Mam.

And give them strength.

And bless the ones who sent flowers.

And bless the insurance man.

And bless the bodies departed from us Lord.

With Rachel's mother eyes shut tight chipping in and reminding the good Lord where them bodies are resting just so he don't have to go looking with all his angels and cherubs.

They're in the chapel of rest Lord.

Over in Trallwn.

The little yellow building.

Second door on the right as you go in.

But they'll be over here tomorrow morning Lord.

We leave the house at half-past ten.

Making you feel for certain as how Ieuan Watts definitely got influence up there. And as how at half-past ten God will be in Cilfynydd on the dot.

Hearing him finish that prayer with an amen so loud you think they can hear it next door if it wasn't for the rain bashing at the window panes like some mad sod is shovelling dried peas against the glass. And seeing him sit back on the sofa thumbing through that twisted exercise book.

You could have three hymns.

Three would be all right.

If you think so Mister Watts.

Two at the house here.

First and last verses only.

Don't take up too much time.

Just first and last.

And one at the graveside.

Abide with Me for that one.

Is Abide with Me all right?

They'll know the tune.

I don't mind Abide with Me.

We never got to church much Mister Watts.

Chapel I am.

Don't want a church service do you?

And when he asks that question you feel as if he have asked you for a rubber to rid your name from the Lamb's Book of Life. So you tell him no and as how chapel will be fine. Hearing him clear his throat and start singing this hymn with a richness and sincerity of voice you find spellbinding if preachers go about casting spells.

For ever with the Lord.

Amen so let it be.

Life from the dead is in that word.

'Tis immortality.

Here in the body pent.

Absent from him I roam.
Yet nightly pitch my moving tent
A day's march nearer home.
Do you know it?
        No.
Might be nice for the house.
There's plenty will know the tune.
I'll bring my leaflets with the words.
Just first and last.
Not to take up time.
The Lord have got a clock.
And each of us got a timing.
Stands to reason.
We must keep our schedules.

With the clock on the mantelpiece chiming out eleven o'clock
above the clatter of the rain. And the old man licking his thumb
for turning the pages of that exercise book all slow and deliberate
like the good Lord have given him an option or two on them
schedules he told you about. Noticing little bits of paper lying
here and there between the dog-eared pages with scribblings and
messages same as IOU's and receipts concerning God's work you
reckon. Picking one up as it falls on the mat and handing it back
to him noticing the words *Plaid Cymru* with the green triangles
they use as a badge stamped across the backing. And wondering
what he got to do with Welsh nationalism and whether or not it
is true that *Plaid Cymru* have got as strong a grip around the hearts
of Welshmen as you've heard it said. And feeling that from now
on you will think about holiness and Christ whenever you see
them triangles.

Not having a headstone are you?
        No.
A plaque is just as nice.
And the Saviour don't mind.
But what will you put on it?
        Rest in peace I expect.
        Or God is love.
I'll tell the men at the masons.

They got them all ready made up.

Black or white?

One long one or two small ones?

How will they be buried?

Side by side my son.

More of a union that way.

More of a bond.

One long plaque.

Black marble.

And he writes it down in that precious book using this kid's green wax crayon he have pulled out from inside his ratting hat. Making you feel as how things are safe in his hands.

Hearing this voice from Rachel's mother all quiet nearly a whisper so you feel like you got to clear your throat telling him

I thought the Lord's My Shepherd might be nice.

You can't have first and last.

It don't make much sense.

It's very popular.

We could sing it quick.

I'll write it down.

And soon he have made a little list of the items he got to chase up for the funeral. Watching him press this paper strip marker between the pages of that exercise book. Rolling it up again and shoving it down the front of his trousers where he keeps that office.

So he kneels once more and gets you praying. Thanking God for his blessing and guidance throughout the arrangements. And Rachel's mother nudging you at the end to follow his amen with one of your own.

Watching him adjust them bike clips around his ankles. And the creak and squeak of oilskins as he zips the front of his coat. Wheeling his bike out into the street. Into the rain as a black and white moggy sprints bedraggled from under one parked car to the next. Lurking hungry for small drain rats seen sometimes racing along the gutters when Wood Street is quiet.

Thank you for coming Mister Watts.

Good-night boy.

God bless.

Right.
        I forgot one thing.
        You never said.
Yes?
        What was they called?
What?
        The mother and child.
Rachel and Miriam.
Rachel was my wife.
        I must put it down.
        Good-night boy.

[17]

Standing soggy-footed with the rest around the open graves at eleven sharp. Feeling the sting and cold of early January drizzle pocking into your face. Tasting the freshness of that rain as you lick your lips. Noticing distinct as how Lew have not come deliberate. Thinking his anger must be great to stretch beyond the sympathy in death showed by sixty or seventy others standing there even maybe for the sake of appearances. Some women's faces but mainly men holding their caps and trilby hats by their sides. Standing soaking from the wet earth and from the wet sky. Catching their death as the coffins get put down on canvas guide belts. And the deadened smack of each as they splatt on the water built up at the bottom of the graves.

Staring at Ivor and Haydn and Len and Beano and Mad Ike and the rest huddled shivering in their macs with best suit trousers poking out from underneath in reverence for the occasion. Standing empty-faced looking at the grass not moving. Not a movement. Except Ivor who glances at the clouds with his one good eye. And then at you. And then at the grass.

And Uncle Albert standing stiff. Erect for all his seventy-two years. Apart from the rest out of habit. Conditioned on purpose by the army who made him an RSM for twenty years with the South Wales Borderers so that now he is repelled automatic by any grotty bunch of human beings unless they are standing in ranks ready for inspection. And mister I can tell you for nothing as how Albert is waiting for a volley to be fired across them graves.

Remembering the commotion of ten years past when Albert never paid his water rates and the council cut him off. And him there in his bungalow up Graigwen on the telly and in the newspapers and everything. Telling this gawping world as how it was the duty of the council to supply every living soul with water free of charge since it happened to be a gift from heaven in the first place and too bloody dear in the second. Telling them all straight. And telling them as how not a drop would pass his lips unless it came from out of the spout of his own back kitchen tap.

Seeing his photo in the *South Wales Echo* front page and in the *Western Mail* page three. Wearing them two rows of medals he got from the army. With the whole thing going on like a crusade for nearly a week. Till it turned all serious. Or till this gawping world understood how determined Albert could be. Getting weaker and drier as the days went by. Till his lips was all bulging and one of his eyes stayed shut. Lying there photographed on his pit with this load of letters and cards around him from different quarters. Till he lost his powers of speaking on account of the sores on his swollen tongue. And poking out that tongue more for comfort than for defiance. Letting it loll there over his bottom lip same as a brown coat hanging over a chair.

Hearing and seeing this handful of doctors talking on the telly and saying as how Albert was dying from thirst and massive dehydration. And as how it was only his spirit that kept him going.

With this petition signed by the residents and rate-payers of Graigwen and district being handed over to the chairman of the Taf-Fechan Water Board. And him bleating on about how the whole thing never had nothing to do with him and as how he didn't want Uncle Albert on his conscience just because he'd rather die than pay his rates same as everybody else. And the British Legion starting legal proceedings against him and the rest of Taf-Fechan Water Board on a charge of murder. Till somebody somewhere turned on the mains and Uncle Albert got his water back.

Staring at him standing there in the drizzle still apart from the common herd. And reckoning as how he must have won through in the end. Not hearing a dicky bird about them water rates ever since he got out of hospital. Giving this great Vee sign on the front page of the *Daily Mirror* in his hour of triumph never mind the likes of you and me who carry on forking out twice yearly same as we would if the council up and rated the very air we breathe.

It has come to the notice of the Rating Department that for the period X_3GW_6 to X_3GW_9 inclusive you used up more cubic inches of air than was assessed by the Ratings Office for the same period last year. You are therefore in excess of your valuation for this year and subject to statutory surcharge as per receipt. If said surcharge remittance is not received by the 24th of this month the Air Board will have no alternative but to block up one of your nostrils.

And bald old Islwyn Protheroe handing out the hymn sheets like a schoolboy in assembly. Looking all important and feeling extra special on account of having a job to do at a famous funeral. Wearing his County Councillor badge on the lapel of his mac so people can see he got quality as well as hymn sheets. With that quality running in the shape of a seat on the Education Committee down at Cardiff where they got this habit of appointing his sons and daughters as headmasters and headmistresses of schools large and small throughout Glamorgan.

With just a few bitter MA's and BA's complaining amongst their kind as how old Islwyn went and had a comprehensive school built the other side of Ponty just for Sid his eldest who only passed five subjects at O level and managed to scrape a teaching certificate on the second attempt at Caerleon. And who only taught backward children for three years in Birmingham before becoming headmaster of the comprehensive his dad built. But mister I can tell you for nothing as how them BA's and MA's and experts had better shut their mouths in case old Islwyn hears their talkings on account of him having a terrible temper once he gets going. And quite likely to make them all redundant to requirements if he got a mind. And him having this load of experience in that direction being charge-hand for thirty-five years down at the bone works in Rhydyfelin before he taught himself to read pretty good and got this sense of mission about education and the rest.

Except for every one of them teacher flowers who complains all bitter about Islwyn there are ten more who know how to knock on his door after dark. Who know how to be humble in his generous presence. And who know how to beg and scrape for the crumbs he got to offer in the way of promotion. With them being the ones who get on in Islwyn's world of schooling. Dotted around this town of Pontypridd. Headmasters headmistresses registrars and deputies all of his making overnight so to speak.

Remembering how Rachel and yourself spent hours in the bedroom window clocking the dark shadows and shapes sneaking up Wood Street towards number hundred and four where he lives the night following the death of Harry Williams headmaster of Gwyn Street Juniors who dropped dead that very afternoon caning a girl for spitting at a teacher. Seeing them calling one after the other all anonymous and humble getting in a quick scrape before Harry's corpse went cold.

You don't know me Mr Protheroe.

I'm a teacher down Treforest.

I hold the Labour Party card.

Yes I'm fully paid up.

I done my emergency training thirty years ago.

I never fogged up my brains with extra knowledge.

I can handle the little dears all right.

What they need is the stick isn't it?

I can hit good.

Feel that arm sir.

Remember me remember my face.

With old Islwyn keeping some of them standing there on the doorstep as he chewed his bacon sandwich. Letting them ramble on about how good they are. And about how they got twenty years experience and two degrees and diplomas from Oxford and a vast history of classroom and administrative success in a whole long list of different schools and so on. And old Islwyn nodding wisely and flicking his braces against his vest in that habit he got. And shutting the door. And opening it again for the next. But knowing all the while as how his daughter Millie will get Gwyn Street even though she don't yet know poor Harry have gone to his maker.

And this big fuss being kicked up by quite a few with ambitions waiting all anxious for the job to get advertised. Sitting at home reading up all the latest crap on teaching and modern methods from books and things. Waiting shivering with excitement same as whippets on a short lead. Fancying their chances and brushing up their credentials. Not dreaming for one minute as how the headship of Gwyn Street have already been advertised twice (once in the *Nottingham Evening Post* and once in the *East Sussex Gazette*) and as how a short list of three have been drawn up and as how Millie Protheroe is on that list after this one year of experience in Upper Boat Infants. And as how she have been made headmistress of Gwyn Street Juniors by this unanimous vote down at County Hall.

And you and Rachel having a good laugh at all the long teacher faces walking about when they hear the news. Reckoning as how Millie should run Gwyn Street pretty good at the end of the matter seeing as how her deputy is this double honours whizz-kid from Cardiff who been teaching for years and years under Harry Williams and never a slur against his name.

Seeing old Islwyn hand a soggy leaflet to Ivor who smoothes the rain off it and smudges all the print before letting the thing drop to the grass like he is looking for an excuse not to sing. But Ieuan Watts striking up Abide with Me before Ivor got time to make up his mind. And seeing them one-eyed lips move open and closed as the rest bring him into the tune.

With Islwyn caught napping before he have given out all the hymn sheets and rushing around the last few in a kind of soaking flap to join in breathless himself half-way through verse one.

Thinking as how you never heard Rachel sing a hymn once in her life being not surprising seeing as you never went with her to chapel. Not even when she came over all religious for about three months after Miriam got born. Regretting that now on account of not being able to sing the tune right like plenty who can standing around the graves.

I am a heathen Lord.

I got no voice for hymns.

> Pretend to sing O my lamb.
> They are all clocking you.
> Keep your gob moving isn't it.

Putting in your muted two penn'orth and staring at the hymn sheet limp and dripping between fingers that have started to come clean with washing since they had a rest from digging down the Deep Maritime. Wiping the rain spots off Abide with Me and seeing the words come blurred so they run in dark streamlets down the page and vanish back into the earth.

Hearing the last chords of that miserable stirring hymn echo shakily into the leaning side of Paradise Hill where they are swallowed secretly by the trees and ferns and bushes and birds and other live things that have heard it all before. And have heard your tongue telling words of sweetness and love to Melody through the first summer of worship together. Stretched there beneath the cedars when the wind blew only gentle up from Tonkin's Wood. And the pulverising scent of bluebells heavy on each tantalising gust. Through her hair. Across the ruffles on her dress front. And the donkey-grass pillow swaying now and then around her resting head. A private hill. A secret hiding place. For an hour. And sometimes longer.

Last night I kissed you in my mind.

Were you thinking of me?

Lew was upstairs in bed.

And I kissed you Ben.

It was real.

I nearly cried.

> Don't ever cry Melody.
> Was it so real?

As real as this.

And I counted the hours.

There was sixteen left.
        And now we are here.
We are here.
Touch me all over.
Press me.
Mark me.
I want it to last.
        I know.
        I get that feeling.
I want to be your wife.
Your wife your wife.
        My wife.
        Now you are my wife.
        Just for now.
        Just here.
I belong to no one else.
No one.
They are all dead.
Hearing Ieuan Watts sniff long and loud up his dribbling
Baptist nose. Seeing him adjust them year-of-dot tortoise-shell
glasses he must have got on the National Health when they came
out first. Same as them yellow worn-down teeth he clicks firmer
into place when he is ready for saying his prayers. And him stand-
ing there over the coffins with his exercise book out and opened.
Gasping in this deep breath and setting back his shoulders like
his voice is going to carry up to the very gates of Heaven itself.
    We commend these souls to you Lord.
Knowing as how you took them for a reason.
Whatever that reason might be.
Though it is hard to understand.
Amen.
Perhaps you had a vacancy O Lord.
For the little one I expect.
And perhaps you thought you'd better have Mam as well.
Like for a bit of company Lord.
Till the baby settled down up there.
Amen.

I expect you got plenty for them to do O Lord.
Perhaps you got them glorifying you right now.
Perhaps they are shouting loud hosannas.
And hailing thy blessed name even as we stand here.
Amen.
There must be plenty to do up there O Lord.
We know as how you got a big place.
You sent your boy Jesus down and he told us isn't it.
He told us as how you got many mansions built there.
And we know there must be maintenance to do.
We understand O Lord.
We know as how you need helpers.
And some of us down here are always willing.
You only got to say O Lord.
We know you will call us when it is time.
Them amongst us who do love you.
Amen.
Amen for God is love.
So don't worry O Lord.
For we know as how Rachel and Miriam are in safe hands.
We lambs know we can rely on the Good Shepherd.
Thank you Lord.
Amen.
And bless the one left behind Lord.
Bless the boy Ben in his hour of loss.
And the girl's mother who do miss her terrible.
But especially the boy who have been good to them.
Give him a blessing and smile upon him.
Warm his heart up Lord.
And give him a chance of happiness.
He is young Lord.
Young in body and spirit.
Bless him and the memory of his departed family.
May his bread be ever fresh.
Amen and amen.
With that rain driving harder so it clop clops against the canvas
cover on that earth mound they left to one side excavating the

holes. And Ieuan Watts turning back one corner of the covering to take up a handful of muck. Splaying that muck on the coffins between them ashes to ashes dust to dust words pretty damn quick before his voice gets lost to the coming storm.

Clocking these two old-fogey men standing to one side on the gravel path behind the crowd. Dressed in black oilskins with spare sacking over their heads. Hiding their grave-digging spades up under their capes out of reverence. But a wisp of fag smoke coming from inside one of the oilskins out through the cape neck and whisked away by the rising wind. And knowing there is no reverence at all.

Taking his bloody time.
    Bloody nigh frozen.
He have said ashes to ashes.
Why don't they all bugger off?
    Always makes sure.
    He got to be certain.
Have he?
    Ieuan Watts.
    Buried my mother.
Is that right?
    Takes his time.
    Makes certain.
Certain?
    They are gone.
Where?
    Up.
How can he tell?
    Never says.
    Can't say how he knows.
    But he do.
    He knows.
    Won't ever leave a grave.
    Not till he's certain.
He's turning to go.
    They must be gone up.
    He must be certain.

[18]

With heads and faces and some heads without faces (or none you ever saw before) filling every room not to mention the passage the stairs the landing and even out the back. Women dressed bulging in black frocks and clean pinnies smelling of mothballs and Vick and sherry standing everywhere feeling more posh than mournful. And old men and bald men and half a dozen with shining pink faces smelling of bitter. Out of their element and wolfing sand-wiches and olives and anything with a plate underneath it because it is there. Chew chew gulp gulp dribble and belch amongst the smell of cooked ham and boiled ham and all the other bits you can carve off a dead pig. With Rachel's mother standing bum to fire surrounded by ladies in waiting. Hatchet-faced razor-mouthed ladies who know what it's all about. Experts at feeding mourners well and sending them home with nothing much to grumble about. Clocking around hawk-eyed picking out hangers-on who never did their stint at the graveside and who don't deserve maybe more than one ham sandwich and perhaps a Marie biscuit before they gets told the way it is with funeral food around this town.

Was you at the graveside Ianto Pugh?

No.

I got this cough.

This spread is not for you then.

Get off home and don't come back.

Don't mind me telling you do you?

No.

I was going.

Past the ordinary old to where the very old very cold sit with their coats on around that long table in the front parlour where the fireplace is bricked in for stopping the draught coming down the chimney. Staring at them. Two dozen or more dug up from somewhere to give the whole gathering quality and wisdom. Sat there staring at their brown plates. Foggy-eyed and highly senile waiting day in day out for the worm or hypothermia to catch them napping. Staring at them. And them at you. And then back at their plates. And on each plate two tomatoes one slice of ham plenty of cucumber discs a lettuce leaf and three pickled onions to shake up long sleeping taste buds in two dozen or more tired mouths. With a bottle of Heinz salad cream every four plates. And a jar of sliced beetroot every six.

Thought she'd have put something hot.

I could do with something hot.

Something to warm my insides.

I can't sleep for the cold.

Thought she'd have warmed us up.

> They got a fire in the kitchen.

> And one in the middle room.

I like to see a flame.

I got to have a flame.

> You'll see flames soon enough Abe Watkins.

> Don't worry about seeing flames.

What do you mean Sarahnna?

What's all this about seeing flames?

> After what you did to Millie.

> No way to treat a tidy little wife.

I never done nothing Sarahnna.

> You was out when she passed away.

> Everybody knows you was out.

> You had no business being out.

I was only out the back.

I got to go out the back now and again.

The flush was stuck.

> You was out.

> The Devil looks after his own.

> Don't worry about seeing flames.

> They got all your sins listed up there.

> You'll see a flame all right Abe Watkins.

She was dying for months.

How did I know to stop in?

She may have lingered.

I thought she was lingering.

With very old talk that have been going on for years still going on about things that have passed years even before you was born. And them mouths stopping nasty words for minutes on end as wobbly teeth or shrivelled gums get chewing on the ham. As throats clogged with age and cucumber swallow hard and slow and painfully lumpy in a front parlour more chilled with bitter rememberings than draught escaping from under the oilcloth.

Pass me the onions.

    I'm not passing you no onions.

I haven't got an onion.

I can't reach like I used to.

    You can reach when it suits you.

Not as far as the onions.

Reckoning as how if you live that long you hope some social worker will come along all quiet and tip you into a bag and put you somewhere out of the way. Or maybe a double-decker bus from Taff Ely could do the trick if you could get as far as the edge of the road. Or a bottle of Codeines or a bellyful of Domestos. Or a night-ride to nowhere on the back of an unbroken stallion.

But you hope you won't linger. And you hope your mind don't go bang.

Clocking Ieuan Watts sitting on the stair balancing a plate on his knees and salting a tomato. Wondering if he been paid yet.

Have you been paid yet Mister Watts?

Have Rachel's mother seen you right?

How much do we owe you?

    Normally four pounds.

    Except this time there was two.

    But I can't take eight.

    Give me six.

Take the eight Mister Watts.

    No.

Go on take it.

You done all right.

    It's the Lord's work boy.

    Thank you thank you.

    I'll take the seven.

Thank you thank you.

Just the seven.

On past him up the stairs and across the landing to the bedroom you been using since you got out of hospital. Closing the door behind you and listening to the hubbub seeping up muffled from downstairs. And the sound of laughter somewhere out on the back garden path. A child's laugh. And a girlish scream. And the sound of that zinc bath tub being knocked off the nail on that outside wall.

We'll be OK here Ben.

Mam says we can stop on for a bit.

Till we get fixed up with our own place.

This is a nice room.

This have been my room ever since I can remember.

Good view Rachel.

You can see the tips.

When the mist goes you can see Glyncoch.

A good view.

Staring at her sitting on the edge of the bed wearing that pink outfit she bought special for the wedding. And that bloody daft half-moon hat stuck on her head with one of the yellow embroidered flowers flopping untidy off the side tangling with her rich black hair grown shoulder length same as that piece in *Peyton Place* and half the other girls around this copy-cat town. But looking pretty even though her front have started bulging a fair bit. Sitting there fresh from the Courthouse Street registry where you just signed the book.

You married me then?

You never had to.

I said that didn't I?

I never made you.

I wanted to.

I'm glad.

I'd do it again.

You got to say that.

It's done.

I'm glad.

And me.

Watching her undo the front of that suit and lolling back on the bed alongside her. Staring at the ceiling where the damp have etched a brown-stained face with three eyes. And all of them clocking you and her. A tidy room. A room with a view.

There's a place going five doors down.

They only want four thousand.

    I know.

With her big brown eyes like saucers staring at you there on the bed beside her for the first time in a proper house with nothing to hide. And you kiss her long. And she rolls on top of you wriggling hard for them feelings of nearness.

We could move away Ben.

It don't matter about that house.

We don't have to stick around Ponty.

We could live anywhere.

Even Port Talbot.

    Port Talbot?

Or Swansea or Cardiff.

We could live in Neath.

    You said Port Talbot.

I meant anywhere.

We could live anywhere.

It don't matter about that house.

It don't matter about Ponty.

    It do.

    I like it around here.

    I don't mind Ponty.

Nor me Ben.

It's where you was brought up.

It's that more than anything.

    The both of us.

Yes.

With her gone now and so rare you can hardly believe it. Being same as a dream. Staring at that bed decked out in the same orange quilt. And that same brown-stained face with three eyes looking down like it was yesterday. Telling her

We can buy that house.
I don't mind if it's OK.
    It's a good house.
    They done it out.
All right then Rachel.
Get it fixed up.
As if you might expect her to walk in any minute wearing that selfsame bloody daft half-moon hat all wicked looking and randy ready for anything. Being lies all lies and not likely to happen this side of Judgement Day. Go ask the painters working five doors down. Go ask that hubbub underneath.

[19]

Till the last floorboard have been nailed back in place. Till the final thumbprint is squashed determined into putty not yet dried. And the last lick of paint is feathered round the back door latch. Making your house a house again. With a new telly from Rediffusion and all the rest from the Co-op. Being returned payment of their insurance money at the end of the matter and the proper thing to do.

Except above it all and the stink of turps and newness there is the stink of burning. It is there. It clings. Coming and going when the time is right and the wind is ready for catching that awful flavour. Fingering out a grain or an ash or a long hidden bubble of paint the workmen have missed. And bringing that flavour to your nostrils same as some kind of epitaph for Rachel and Miriam so you got to take notice. So you can't forget. Not for all that long.

I still smell burning.
It's here Beano.
Can you sniff it?
    Bound to be.
    Bound to be.
They used enough paint.
I seen the requisition.

You'd have thought isn't it.

Watching Beano going around tapping everything with his biro like he can get some kind of message running up his arm same as locomen with their hammers tapping wheels. Tapping the walls. Tapping the firegrate. And the mantelpiece. And the sideboard. And the light switch.

Bit of a botch.

Can't get the craftsmen.

Got to make do.

    Thought it was all right.

    Looks well done.

What's behind it though?

Did they get down to the stone?

There's a feeling isn't it?

    I can still smell burning.

    Just now and then.

No pride.

    In waves.

Quick lick.

Then hand out for the money.

That's how it is.

Bit of a botch.

Bound to get the smell.

It'll be on the stone.

Bound to.

    It's all right though.

    When you know what it is.

I'm not saying.

They done their best.

Bit of a botch.

But I seen worse.

    I seen a lot worse.

Considering they done it in two months.

You can't argue with two months.

I seen a lot worse.

The smell will go.

    Will it?

Bound to.
Bound to.
    Might wear off.
Bound to.
Bound to.

[20]

Blowing along Taff Street frozen half numb in a gusty March
wind. Wondering if it will snow before morning. With ice-cold
flecks of something or other nicking your face now and again from
out of the orange swirls of the street lamps shaking nervous high
above your head. And that street deserted till chucking out time.
Hurrying on ahead of this following scurry of chip wrappings and
paper cartons and fag packets and other gutter trash swirling
around your feet and up into your face. Till you get to Joe's place.
And the warmth from twenty radiators and a hundred or more
pairs of lungs socking that frigid tightness away from your body
as you push past through the haze through the gloom up to the
sandwich bar.

    You got a crowd tonight Len.

    Give us a ham roll.

        Always the same this time Friday night.

        Mostly Poles.

        Money burning holes.

        Foreign bastards.

        We only got cheese.

    Cheese then.

        Heard about your trouble.

        Pity that.

        Sudden like.

    A bit quick.

    Squinting round through the murk but knowing no man's face
except Mad Ike lit up like a beacon on Table Four. Cueing careful

for the blue. And playing this nigger boy they call Sugar according to Len.

Comes from Cardiff.

Never been here before.

Came up this morning.

Been here all day.

Don't smoke nor eat nor drink.

Plays good.

> It's his height.

> Christ look at his arms.

> He don't need no rest.

Like hose-pipes.

He got a good reach.

Him and Ike is even.

> Even?

> Mad Ike even?

Seventh game.

They won three each.

They'll be even on the game.

If Ike gets the blue.

And Ike gets the blue. Stretching his back and chalking up all serious for the next red. With everything safe as far as you can work out. Being that kind of game.

Big pot.

I'm holding it.

Got it in a box under here.

They been doubling.

> Is that right?

> Seven games?

About three hundred pounds.

I reckon about that region.

About that.

About three.

With Haydn perched same as some kind of sparrow-hawk on this rickety stool marking the board. And holding the side bets in both his back pockets judging by the size of his bum. Hearing him tell Ike good shot as the cue ball rolls safe.

He been drinking too heavy lately.

He got the shakes.

　　Ike don't drink heavy.

Since Christmas.

Seeing Ike brush back his hair with the back of his hand leaving this faint sweat smear across that wrinkled forehead. Noticing as how he have gone a lot more grey since you saw him last. And older in the face. Same as an ageing dog who might alter from normal into something fat and worn out in just a couple of months depending on his breeding. Mad Ike puts you in mind of that.

Clocking Sugar poke the white out gentle from the cush to fluke the last red. And he pots the yellow and the green and the brown and the blue. Leaving Ike with a simple shot on the pink and Haydn all agitated.

No good Ike.

You are behind.

You need a snooker.

　　I know I know.

　　Shut up.

And Ike got to play safe again. With the nigger grinning all relaxed and young-looking. Knowing he have outclassed and out-lasted this old man. And as how the pot is his very own if he can take the pink. With a big game being best of seven up Joe's or any other snooker hall you ever played in where the shooting is for money and eff all to do with love. Feeling Len pull your arm pointing to the cheese roll.

Ike have cocked it Ben.

Watch a man lose.

　　That nigger is good.

Better you mean.

　　Better then.

Watching him take the pink in the centre left from a cush cannon he could afford to risk. Taking the pot from Len all smiles. Handing him five pounds in singles for his trouble. And leaving quick for Cardiff same as any other pro who got better things to do than stop and talk.

With Mad Ike melted back into the gloom beaten for a load of money so you only got Haydn to watch handing out his bits to the punters round the sides. And him showing a dead loss for the first time in years.

Bloody nigger was lucky.

All niggers is lucky.

They got it born in them.

Look at Cassius Clay.

Look at Louis Armstrong.

They all got fucking luck.

A white man got no chance.

Stands to reason.

And him coming up to the bar asking for a Wonderloaf cob with butter. Standing there all crabby like he just seen the error of his ways or something. Bitching at Len for keeping stale bread. And staring at you same as something evil.

Your brother wants you.

He haven't finished yet.

He haven't started.

    What he want Haydn?

Your guts.

And he'll bloody have them.

    What for?

What for?

His wife that's what for.

He haven't finished yet.

Letting things settle.

    Settle?

He heard about your trouble.

Knows all about the fire.

Won't kick a man when he's down.

Letting things settle I expect.

But he still wants you.

I mean you can't forget isn't it.

She never come back.

    She don't want him.

He wants the kid.

He blames you for the kid.

Not seen sight of them.

    Nor me.

He knows that.

It don't matter.

He wants your guts.

And he'll bloody have them.

    No chance Haydn.

Can I tell him that?

Can I say you give me a message?

Can I say he got no chance?

    If you like.

    If he wants to settle things.

    He knows where I live.

    You can tell him that.

[21]

With that *New Inn* crowd thick and swallowing hard down the throats of cockney lads and men early in Ponty keen for making a mint or two next day. Booked in as usual on the second and third floors of that one-star hotel so they can get an early start to trading in the morning. So they can get them English Jewboy teeth stuck into simple valleys wallets and purses brought down innocent from Porth and Ton-Pentre all eager for bargains in the shape of china tea-sets Adidas bags (plastic looking like leather) for the kids so they can be same as other kids daps (cheaper than Woolworth's) fresh-cut flowers ties second hand filthy books from Germany parallels A-lines from Polikoff's up Treorchy handbags shoes parkas quilts curtain oddments french letters and birthday cards.

Nudging through their knotted cockney bodies ponging of scent and kosher snacks packed by Momma back in London. Towards Gwen Ann looking girlish and tipsy now that the weekend have come at last.

Pint of tankard Gwen Ann.

And a glass with a handle.

All the handles are out.

Smirnoff straight then.

A double.

Getting jostled by this big Asian from the watch and bracelet stall. Seeing him pull out this roll of notes looking like twenties and reckoning he must be carrying around two thousand pounds or more in his hip pocket. Seeing him peel off one of them mauve notes slapping it on the bar counter.

Can you change that love?

No.

Large scotch.

On the slate then.

Room forty-three.

Have one yourself.

Thank you.

Watching him knock back his drink in one gulp and melt back into that cigar-stinking group of darkies standing laughing outside the Ladies. Pushing yourself away from the bar with one hand over the top of your drink so others can make their orders. Wondering about the rest of the pubs you know around Ponty. And wondering if they might be half as full as the *New Inn*. Reckoning a man got a right to sitting down even if it is Friday night.

And leaning against the juke box some sod have fused on purpose. With the taste of that Smirnoff scorching from the back of your gullet up into the front of your skull. Letting the zip of the stuff mellow into a vague kind of muzziness so even the cigar smoke begins to smell good. And holding up your arm above the crowd so Gwen Ann sees you. Pointing to your glass so she knows to fill another by the time you reach the bar again. Seeing her smile. Seeing her nod.

You drank that quick Ben.

Are you driving?

Not tonight.

Big crowd even for a Friday.

Too big.

Go up to my room if you like.
I'm off in forty minutes.
I got a relief coming.
You want to go up?
    Empty is it?
There's no one coming.
Not tonight.
Go on up.
You want to?

With her room being on the top floor and higher up than you ever imagined the *New Inn* could stretch. So high that you can look down on Taff Street and feel funny even without a gut full of booze. So high up you can look down on Woolworth's being a sight not many men have ever seen. And you wait for her.

Clocking round that room she been living in for years. And her bed all rumpled and slept in with a pillow on the floor. Wondering when she last lay down with Mad Ike beside her. Expecting to find a cube of snooker chalk and a couple of leather tips in the ash-tray but only finding ash and some cotton and an Embassy dog-end.

I brought a bottle.
Smirnoff blue label.
Can't always get it.
Eighty per cent proof.
    You want that neat?
Blows your eyeballs out.
There's lime here somewhere.
How has it been?
    All right.
Do you want me?
    Yes.
Do you think I'm a callous bitch?
If you think that it don't matter.
Not to me.
    No Gwen Ann.
    You are OK.
    I don't think that.

You got to put it somewhere.

If you are a man that makes sense.

You got to use it.

It might as well be me.

I like you anyway.

I like you a lot Ben.

I like you too.

And all the time she is talking she is searching that room for the lime. As if she got to get her intentions straight in the first place on account of not having a load of time for messing about playing daft romantic games before it happens. With Gwen Ann it is a straight question of glands and the excitement of her sexual explosion. Being logical. Being very fair.

I found the lime.

Shall I pull my knickers down?

Feeling this throb of pipes filling and the rattle of water being drawn underneath your feet as some Jewboy draws a bath the next floor down. Cleansing himself you reckon in readiness for killing off them sacrificial lambs from the valleys when they find his market stall in the morning.

You don't have to.

Not yet.

I thought to get ready.

In case you got to go.

That's all right Gwen Ann.

Watching her pour the drinks steady as a rock though you can tell she have had a few already. Half filling two tumblers with that blue half-smoked effect you can find on very expensive glass. And topping them with enough lime to choke the taste bite away. And resting them on the bedside table near the ashtray.

Come and sit here Ben.

It's softer.

Sitting alongside her. Taking the vodka from the table. And shuddering to the first gulp as the impact rocks the back of your eyes.

Christ.

With this faint flicker of a smile coming and going in the

corners of her mouth as she stares at you and touches your hair.

It's a good drink.

You know about drink?

    Not much.

I got a habit with drink.

I don't mind having a habit.

I get very lonely Ben.

Stuck up here.

This can be a lonely room.

    You got it done nice though.

    This is all right.

It's free.

I don't pay rent or anything.

All this stuff is mine.

    It's OK.

Nothing's OK mister.

Not at the end of things.

Not when you are on your own.

You must know about that.

You had time to learn?

Nodding on account of it feeling right to nod. And watching her swallow that blue label in one quick gulp. Wiping her mouth with her frilled pinny as she takes it off unzipping that grey tight skirt and stretching back on the bed wearing just this brown blouse and cord mesh red pants with Love It on the front.

Promise me Ben.

Will you please?

    What?

Make it quick.

Don't torment me.

Promise you won't.

    I don't know Gwen Ann.

    You can't say.

Yes you bloody can.

You know what I mean.

Promise you won't.

All right.

I got a thing about that.

I can't stand tormenting.

I can't bear to wait.

I'll hate you if you do that.

I don't want to hate you.

> Men like to torment.
>
> It's more than one quick bang.
>
> There's more to it than that.
>
> But I promise.

I get scared if I got to wait.

Can you understand that?

> Yes.

And then it don't happen.

It don't bloody happen.

Not for me.

> Did he do that?

What?

My correspondent?

> Him.

All the time.

Now it's over.

After Christmas.

It ended.

Nine years ended.

And she pulls off the rest of her clothes lying naked there on that crumpled bedspread. Noticing as how the line of her breasts is starting to sag in that position with the firmness of youth clean wore out of them. Staring at her body. Still a fair sight by any way of looking. Seeing her turn on her side to stretch out an arm towards you. Taking hold of her hand. And letting her pull you alongside. Gulping off that drink and dropping the glass on the carpet as she unbuckles your belt. Wriggling awkward out of your trousers. And kicking them off.

How did it end Gwen Ann?

Did the pattern break?

> It took nine years.

What?

    To find out about him.

    About his lies.

    My correspondent.

    I loved him.

You can't switch off.

Not after nine years.

Not that sudden.

    A quick thing.

    And it's over.

    He told me lies.

    I kept myself for him.

    A long long time Ben.

    Till the suffering inside was a habit.

    I was jealous of his wife.

    Jealous of him going home to her.

    Women are awful jealous.

Perhaps there was no need.

Not with your correspondent.

    I found out about him.

    It was after Christmas.

    He made a monkey out of me.

    I been a monkey for nine years.

Your choice.

    Not his lies.

    I never knew about his lies.

    You don't look too hard.

    A woman don't look hard.

    I never looked hard.

You got to take it the way it is.

No sense in looking.

    I should have looked hard.

    He got no bloody wife.

With her words giving you a shock in the head. Reckoning all
your life as how you have thought about **Mad Ike** being married.
Nor never suspecting he is on his own. Being not surprising seeing as neither you nor most others around this town knows where

127

he lives. Always thinking it must be the other side of the Old
Bridge in Trallwn or Pont Sion Norton or one of them back
streets up Norton Bridge. If he lives in Pontypridd at all.

It was up Glyntaff cemetery.

It was Boxing Day.

I found out about his lies.

     Why was you there love?

     Was there a funeral?

Christmas Eve he brought me an orchid.

It was a lovely flower.

I am very fond of flowers.

But I knew it wouldn't keep.

Not with the central heating up here.

So I took it to the cemetery.

I got a sister there.

     Have you?

She died when she was eight.

She had leukaemia.

So I thought I'd go.

I don't go often.

Glyntaff gives me the creeps.

I took that orchid for her grave.

     And your correspondent was there?

     You saw him.

He was scraping the moss away.

There was this headstone with a tilt.

And he had a knife.

And he had put flowers.

I could see that.

I was kneeling.

I was out of sight.

I wanted to shout to him.

But I thought better not.

Better not.

And I watched until he went away.

I was nearly frozen.

And I went up to that headstone.

Her name was Ruth.

He always said it was Ruth.

Always referred to her by that name.

He had a wife then?

He was married?

But she was dead.

Twenty years ago.

Reckoning as how you could tell her Mad Ike got cunning all right judging him on snooker alone. Reckoning you could tell her as how he always keeps his best shots for when he needs them. Pulling something out of reserve so to speak. Just to turn the tide his way. Except you just seen him lose a bundle to that nigger. And wondering if he got hooked on a losing streak all of a sudden. And wondering if maybe all them reserves started trickling away once he lost Gwen Ann. Being some kind of judgement at the end of the matter and a lesson he is not too old to learn.

So when he comes to me that selfsame night I tell him.

I am ready for the lying cheating bastard isn't it.

I got this sharp letter-opener dagger from the office.

And I hid the thing under my pillow isn't it.

I am all anger Ben you got to understand that.

I do.

Stands to reason.

You can only take so much.

I'd taken all of it for nine years.

That's how much I took.

All that time being jealous of some bones.

That's all she is after twenty years.

No skin.

No flesh.

Just bones.

So I ask him why don't you marry me I said.

And he gives me this funny look and he laughs.

Why don't you marry me that's what I said.

And he says I got a wife.

And I say I know you got a wife but she is dead.

And he says what sod told you?

And I tell him no sod told me but I seen her grave.

So he don't say nothing.

And I ask him why he don't marry me after my divorce.

And I ask him why he been hanging me about for nine years.

And still he don't say nothing.

So I ask him why don't he marry me next week.

And the bastard tells me straight isn't it.

I don't want you for no wife he said.

That's what he said Ben.

Them was his words.

I don't want you for no wife.

So I stabs him in the arm high up.

And he don't cry out nor nothing.

So I stabs him again in the chest.

And he hits me back arse over head.

But he don't make no sound.

And he walks out of that door still with the dagger in him.

He just walks out Ben.

After all those years he don't say nothing.

I still can't understand any of it.

I never bloody will.

And you just fondle her automatic. And she pulls in close feeling between your legs and gasping little sounds like she got this desperate need for sex. Like it is there and she wants you to know it is there in spite of everything she took from Ike. And she feels good. Her skin feels smooth. And in your mind she don't deserve nothing but the best from any man. Knowing and feeling she will give her best in return. Knowing it.

If I am hurting it is not deliberate.

I am trying to be gentle Gwen Ann.

> You are not hurting me my love.
>
> I would not feel hurt from you.
>
> This is lovely.
>
> This is lovely.

With her wanting coming quick to a climax just like she said it would. And she is ahead of you and she knows it. And you feel her breath holding. And she pushes her thumb inside her mouth.

And she waits for you in an ecstasy of excitement that makes you breathless too. Feeling her fingers dig hard into the back of your neck till she cannot stand the waiting any more. And you are ready with her. And you are together. Rolling over and over on that bed as it happens long and wild till you think you might faint.

In the summer I might leave.

I might leave this town.

You should stay Gwen Ann.

I got a life.

I got proper things to do.

You can do them here.

Not any more Ben.

Not in Pontypridd.

[22]

And it don't snow proper till Saturday afternoon. Being out with Duke on Paradise Hill when them spitting bits you seen for days begin to flower and grow into broad white flakes filling the sky with a murkiness that tells you there will be a heavy fall. Covering and sticking deadening sounds. Silencing the birds for a while till they get the hang of things. Till they see no danger from the gentle bombardment. Making Duke whimper more with excitement than with fear. Letting him cast about for the scent of rabbit or hare. Trotting on in front of you up the scree slope towards the gorse. Using his nose and his eyes. But seeing a hare leap some two hundred yards away before he gets even an inkling of scent. Seeing that dark shape rise and fall through the snow blanket. And calling the lurcher to heel while you point his sharp head in the right direction. Waiting for a second sighting before the snowfall thickens. Seeing that hare leap again this time nearer. Feeling Duke stiffen and his muscles vibrate as he sees it too.

Get him boy.

And he is off like he got springs on his paws. Leaping racing powdering the snow in a straight line towards that hare. And that hare have sensed his coming. Whipping out quick some fifty yards ahead of the dog. Darting weaving changing direction. Working up tremendous speed. Till Duke heads him off. And kills him.

Watching the dog trot back towards you holding his kill firmly between those terrible jaws. And dropping the dead animal at your feet wagging his tail with pride and satisfaction. Looking up at you then down at the hare. Mouth agape. Tongue lolling to one side in a staccato pant.

Good boy Duke.

Go find another.

Go seek.

Go seek.

Picking up the hare and dropping it inside the canvas bag Beano gave you. Opening your duffle coat and letting the bag hang from your belt. Feeling the last minutes of warmth from that creature seeping out against your leg as you follow Duke's tracks across the hill. Wondering if you can catch another before the snow drives you home. And hoping you can on account of Beano's wife needing two for her stewpot by the time she have cut away and cleaned them up. Reckoning as how her stew is the best thing you ever tasted since you was born especially when she cuts off them hunks of homebaked oatmeal bread to go with it. And knowing you got no need to wait for an invitation to supper any Saturday night when there is stew on the go.

Go seek Duke.

Where's them hares?

Go find another.

Following him across the breast of Paradise Hill to where this curving lip melts meadowy into the valley of Nantgarw. And stopping standing there while Duke trots on downwards trying his luck around the banks of the river. Standing there staring at the waves of snow sweeping over from the Barry mountain through the gap towards Cardiff. Transforming the whole scene till even the coal-pit and the dolomite quarries look pretty. Staring at the new whiteness. At the beauty. Hearing only the bubbling river and the muffled swish of traffic sifting through from the motorway beyond.

And a bark. You hear a bark. A lower sound than Duke's. And not as sharp. A big bark from a big dog. And you see it standing there on the other side of the river. A labrador. Not a fighting bark. Not any kind of urgent challenge. Not a playful sound. Just a bark. And a succession of barks as Duke gets the message. Making him jump into the river and swim across to the other bank. Climbing out and shaking himself dry as that labrador comes up close. And they sniff each other. And Duke circles. And confirms that the labrador is a bitch. And that it will take a hell of a lot more than snow to get her off heat.

Giving him a whistle and a shout though he got terrible hearing all of a sudden. And pretends you are not there. With the snow falling heavier till they are both lost from sight. Whistling so hard that your lips hurt. Shouting uselessly against the air.

Good boy Duke.

Come on home.

Except he got no mind to come on home at least not yet. Making your way back across Paradise Hill without him on account of the cold and the snow perishing you inside and out so that you see no point in waiting till he have finished his fruity business with the labrador. And knowing as how he could find his own way home even if he got dropped on the moon.

We only got one hare Beano.

Duke got fed up.

Saw this labrador.

Wouldn't come.

    Bitch I expect.

    Duke been funny all week.

Left the sod with her.

    He'll be back.

    Give him till morning.

    Knows what he's on that dog.

    Look at this hare.

    Not a tooth mark.

Watching Beano examine that hare all over for damage or disease. Letting the thing swing to and fro by its ears in front of the fire.

133

Sometimes they got glands.

Got to watch them then.

Can't cook a hare with glands.

Sets off a taste right through.

This one's OK though.

You can tell by the balance.

See that balance?

And he carries it out the back kitchen where his wife can be heard chopping the vegetables with her magic knife.

You had a visitor when you was out.

    Visitor?

Knocking your door.

Then she went away.

Wife saw her knocking.

    Her?

    What kind of her?

Nigger girl isn't it.

Wife saw her knocking.

But she never stopped around.

You know who it was?

    Her name is Melody.

    I know her.

With Beano nodding all intelligent like everything been explained to him. Being more concerned about the way that hare might cook at the end of the matter than with any dark-faced woman who comes knocking at your door.

But it have shocked you all right. Reckoning in the back of your mind as how Melody is all set up in foreign parts by now. With maybe a flat in London or Birmingham or even abroad. Thinking as how you might definitely see her again one day in the future. Might see her again a long time off. But not quite so soon. It is the knowing that she have trod in Wood Street that very morning what shocks you. The knowing that she is back in Pontypridd.

Staring out of your parlour window just as it gets dark. Staring at the snow thick on the pavements outside. Hearing the crunch of car tyres biting at the gritted rock-salted road. Wondering if it will snow all night. Wondering if she will come back again to your house.

Sitting staring there out of your window for an hour or more till you see Beano standing outside calling for you to go boozing with him down the non-Political. And telling him yes. And pinning this note to your front door just in case Melody calls. Telling her Key under mat love Ben. And not knowing what kind of things to hope for.

I might have twenty pints tonight.

That's the way I feel Ben.

    Do you no good Beano.

Snow always makes me go like that.

Goes to my head so to speak.

Lovely stuff snow.

Seeing him pick up this handful and roll it into a ball. And he got this grin going taking up the bottom half of his face. And he throws it all of a sudden hitting this old man in the neck on the other side of the street. Hitting him so hard he don't know whether he is coming or going. Going into funny shapes there against the wall clawing slush and snow out from the inside of his collar. And cursing the two of you up in heaps.

  What you do that for Beano?

    You got to isn't it.

    That's what snow's for.

    You got to when you gets the chance.

    Before you know it you'll end up like him.

    He got no lead in his pencil mister.

    One day we'll be targets same as him.

    I won't mind so much.

    Not once I had my turn.

    You got to isn't it.

Letting Ernie Smallman sign you in down the non-Political same
as he pegs you off for work down the Deep Maritime. Reckoning
as how if you can outlive him he will be there by them pearly
gates with his clipboard and pencil waiting to sign you into
Heaven.

Many in tonight Ern?
Not many Beano.
Snow keeping them by the fire.
Pick up later I expect.
Usually get a flood.
Once the film have finished.

Going through into the long downstairs room they spent a
fortune on decorating with Scandinavian planking and copper.
Wondering how long it might be before them fitments go absent
one dark and light-fingered night seeing as how the price of scrap
copper is always steady not to mention high.

Clocking round the tables looking for butties who owe you
pints and seeing the whist players up the far end hoping for tricks
and black deuces. Arguing about who is supposed to call in the
next round. With the same old men time and time again cheating
at buying and cards. Like they have always cheated at everything
even when they was young from marbles to paying the rent.

I bought the last round.
Just after the war.

And one-eyed Ivor near the table skittles supping a brown ale
getting on a skinful shaking a finger at you and grimacing being
the same as a wave and a smile in normal-looking men. So you
wave back and he gurgles off his pint. Crossing to the bar counter
ready for another. And he got his coat off and his sleeves rolled high
same as usual showing off his Death before Dishonour tattoo on
one arm with a dagger going through a skull and First Battalion
Royal Welch Fusiliers on the other surrounded by roses and a
snake. And he is staring at you in that way he got so you feel

like shoving half a pound of pig's muck into his chops. Staring back with that thought clear in your mind hoping your eyes can give him the message.

Have a pint on me.

You and Beano.

I done my hobble today.

And judging by the size of that roll of notes he pulls out from inside his belt that hobble have done him proud.

Been flogging handbags Ivor?

Busy on the market?

  All go isn't it.

  Some of us got to work Saturdays.

You done all right.

  That's commission that is.

  Like piece work isn't it.

  What are you having boys?

Two bitters.

Club draught if it's on.

And it is on. And Ivor shoves two pints towards you and Beano taking another brown for himself.

I saw the black girl today.

  What?

She come to my stall.

I know her of old.

Your brother's wife.

She was buying shoes.

She bought three pair.

I never knew anybody get a supply in.

Not of shoes.

Not all in one go.

Is that right she left him Ben?

  You want to ask Lew.

  We don't bother much.

They said you was having her.

Said you been messing.

And when Ivor says a thing like that he got this natural knack of making the words sound dirtier than unclean. Like you and

Melody been all perverted and abnormal together. Like you done all sorts of filthy things together in foul corners same as animals who got disease and who don't know no better. He makes it sound just like that.

And I heard about you Ivor.

It's all the talk.

I never believed it at first.

But now I know it's true.

What you heard?

They don't talk about me.

They got nothing to say.

What they been saying?

They say as how when no one is looking.

Like when it's all quiet.

When you are on your own.

You got these habits.

What fucking habits?

As how you eat your own crap.

As how you suck your thing.

As how you wear girls' dresses.

As how there's maggots behind your glass eye.

As how you once shagged your mother.

And then your father.

It's all the talk Ivor.

So before he can smash his pint glass in your face you kick him hard up between his legs. And he lets go this scream. Making all them heads turn quick as light. Staring at you (gone all white in the face) and at Ivor gasping and grunting on the Marley tiles. Reckoning he definitely won't get up for a bit. And when he do it won't be for fighting.

With Ernie Smallman coming in holding this chitty foil in one hand and his pencil in the other. Going up to Ivor. Leaning over him and saying

If you sign this Ivor you can have a taxi.

You don't have to fork nothing out.

The club will pay.

You got to sign for it first.

Shoving his chitty foil under Ivor's moaning chops till he gets hold of that pencil all shaky and scribbles his name. Then turning to one side and honking hard so Ernie got to jump like a frog in case that honk goes over his boots. Letting two old men get hold of Ivor and half-dragging half-carrying him out to the transport. And Ernie staring squinting at his chitty.

Not a very good writer isn't it.

Upset I expect.

With Beano staring down frowning at the two pints of bitter lined up on the bar counter. Saying as how it don't feel right to be drinking Ivor's beer round not after you been kicking him all up the knackers and everything.

Feels like hypocrisy isn't it.

We'd be same as hypocrites.

> It don't matter Beano.
>
> Beer belongs to every man.
>
> If it's there it's for drinking.
>
> It don't matter who paid.

Don't it?

> Paying is just a symbol.
>
> Drink up.
>
> It is there.

I bet his balls is sore.

You got a nasty kick in that leg.

> You got to be first.
>
> I seen men who come second.

You did right.

I'm not criticising.

> Drink the beer then.

And you do. Drinking them pints off quick so you can get rid of the last of Ivor hanging around so to speak. And drinking more pints so you can get rid of the taste of the first.

Till it is ten o'clock and Beano is well on the way to twenty. Getting himself tied up with cribbage and these three rejections from Glyntaff.

Gives a man a thirst playing cards.

How many I got to go Ben?

Am I nearly there?

> You are nearly in hospital.

> You got four to go.

> You had sixteen pints.

Jesus I thought I was still thirsty.

No wonder my tongue is all swollen.

I got to have more beer.

My mouth is parched.

> I'll call in the four together.

> Then you'll know where you are.

Make it five.

Then I'm certain isn't it.

A man got to be sure.

So by stop tap Beano have swilled off his twenty pints and one
extra for luck. Wondering where the hell two and a half gallons
of best club bitter have gone to inside his body on account of
never seeing him go to the bogs just once. Reckoning his guts
must be swollen same as a nearly there pregnant mother-woman
or else he got a hollow leg. Except when he stands up from the
cribbage table he don't look no different from usual give or take
a few staggers till he gets a grip of himself.

Have we got time for another?

Let me buy you a pint Ben.

> They have shut the bar.

> I had enough.

> My guts is full.

How many you had?

> Seven.

A little boy's drop.

No wonder you don't grow.

> My guts is full.

> And the money have gone.

I got plenty left isn't it.

Look I got three pound.

I can't go home with three pound.

With that room starting to empty as last orders are swallowed
one by one. Clocking round at the empty glasses. At the empty

chairs. At the empty faces filing past you and Beano leaning against an empty bar with your hands shoved deep into empty pockets.

Staring at him standing there starting to sway as the beer gets a good grip on all his brains. Flowing free there inside that blue-scarred skull. Fermenting more amongst them bits of gristle and thinking tubes you seen in drawings from that medical book your grandpa used to keep the landing door shut tight when the wind got up. Flowing all alcoholic rendered down from the mighty hop. Shoving Beano's blood to one side. Knotting it up into dark corners. Making him start to raise and lower his eyebrows like he always does when he have had his fill. Making his tongue go wonky inside his mouth same as a rubber duck when the wind have leaked away. Scrimping up his nose and cheeks nearly to a point so he begins to look like one of his own ferrets. With a dribble starting in the left hand corner of his drunken chops and the makings of a smile in the right.

I got three pound.

I don't want three pound.

Anybody want three pound?

But there is no man left to hear him except yourself. Pretending to take his money so he can slither home through the snow feeling cleansed and parted from his pay. And the way it was earned.

Getting him home pretty good considering he got to lean heavy. Considering he feels like he only got one leg when you take him up the steps between Ann Street and Wood Street. Dumping him on the snow up the top and seeing he only got one shoe.

What you done with your shoe Beano?

You only got a sock on.

You lost your bloody shoe.

Perhaps I never had it when I come out.

My foot been cold all night.

You was wearing two shoes that's definite.

They was new shoes.

You still got one on.

I must have lost it Ben.

It's gone all right.

141

And the snow have hid it.
You got no hope of finding that shoe.
 Bloody hell.
 I got too much beer inside me.
 I had a good drink Ben isn't it.
I know.
 Who was that black woman?
 The one who come up your house.
Her name is Melody.
She is my brother's wife.
 Have you been messing her?
Yes.
Ivor got it right.
 So you give him a kicking.
Yes.
It got nothing to do with him.
 Quite right.
 Quite right.

Helping him off them steps and down Wood Street. Walking in the road where the snow have not stuck. And him carrying the only shoe he got left under his arm like it is some kind of prize he won on the fair.

You got to come in for stew Ben.

She'll have made it hot.

But you tell him no on account of there being no room in your gut for stew. And you have seen the note gone from your door. And you wonder. You wonder about the whole thing.

[24]

So you think maybe the wind have blown your note away. Clocking round for that bit of paper but seeing nothing only snow. Rubbing your hand up the woodwork and finding the pin still stuck there firm. Pressing the door gentle with your fingers and finding it is off the latch. Searching for your key under the outside mat and finding only dead leaves only a worm only the flagstone.

With no light coming from anywhere inside the house as you go in quiet and shut the door behind you. Standing in the dark of the passage listening with your mouth hanging open trying not to breathe heavy on account of wanting to suck in any other sounds if they are there.

Going through to the kitchen putting on the light. And the middle room and the parlour. But no one is there. And hearing this sound. A slight sound. Just above your head in the back bedroom.

Melody?

I've come home.

Is that you up there?

Melody?

But there is no other sound you can make out. Reckoning as how she may have fallen asleep waiting for you. Looking at your watch and seeing it have stopped at half-past eleven. Climbing the stairs and sniffing hard for a sign of her scent. But smelling nothing except the stink of burnt stone still around reminding you of Rachel and Miriam. That will always be there. You know that much.

Stood there still on the landing. Hardly breathing. Holding the banister with a bit of a tremble going. Staring at the back bedroom door shut and lit up bright by that orange street light coming through from the pine end window nobody can open. Staring at the door and hearing faint in the corner of your brains some barking. Snappy harsh and low. Further down Wood Street or maybe the back lane. Telling you Duke have come back. Just knowing it all in an instant. And in another instant this sound again. This movement sound from inside the bedroom.

Melody?

I am back.

Melody?

Seeing the light go on under the door. And crossing the landing. Opening quick into your bedroom. And staring at Gwen Ann sitting on your bed with her hand on the table lamp.

I heard you come up.

143

I been here an hour.

    What the cowing hell for?

    You got no business in my house.

I saw the note.

Key under mat it said.

So I come in.

    You got no right.

I knew the note wasn't for me.

But I come in anyway.

    What for?

I never been in a proper house for years.

I had a house like this.

Almost the same.

Other side of Neath.

    The note was for somebody else.

    It never meant you.

    You got a bloody cheek.

Shouldn't leave notes.

Nor keys.

It was for her wasn't it?

Your brother's woman.

    No.

I knew it was for her.

When it said love Ben.

You told me you was in love with her.

    That got nothing to do with you.

    You got a bloody cheek.

Staring at her stupid like none of it is real. Except it is real
all right. Staring at her sitting there on your bed still wearing
her sealskin coat and red scarf on account of the cold.

What do you do for warmth Ben?

I nearly bloody froze.

    Never mind what I do.

    You better go Gwen Ann.

    It's getting late.

I come up for a walk that's all.

After stop tap I come up.

I like walking in the snow.
You got to when you got the chance.
You got to isn't it.
    It stopped snowing now.
    You better go.
What for?
We been close isn't it.
You got a nerve.
What you want me to go for?
She's not coming if that's what you think.
    What she?
Melody.
She was in this afternoon.
Her and Lew.
They was friendly.
She gone back to him.
    What?
You got to isn't it.
When there's a kid you got to.
She gone back to him.
He been buying her presents.
She had a bag full of shoes.
    Shoes?
    What's all this about shoes?
I said she would.
It's the kid.
Kids make all the difference.
I never had kids.
A woman should have kids.
I tried hard enough.
With my correspondent.
But he was too bloody clever.
I wouldn't mind having a baby.
I know it hurts.
But I wouldn't mind.
    You should have stuck it out.
    With your husband.

You should have gone back.
If you wanted babies.
That's plain enough.
You are right.
He got married again.
A right little bit of stuff.
She have had two babies.
    See?
I wouldn't want a husband though.
Not him nor anyone.
Not any bloody more mister.
But I wouldn't mind a baby.
Just the two of us.
Maybe a little girl.
They cling more.
Got more feeling.
Just the two of us.
That would be OK.
    You got to go Gwen Ann.
I was good enough last night.
We was close.
    You got no sense Gwen Ann.
    Go home for Christ sake.
    I'm not giving you no baby.
I am no trouble Ben.
You know I am no trouble.
    You got to piss off.
    You are talking crap.
    You don't know much.
    Not at the end of things.
There's no trouble in me.
It's not my nature.
If I have a baby.
If I catch.
Once I am sure.
    Will you fuck off?
    I'm telling you straight.

Once I'm sure.
I'll go away to have it.
I'll stop away for good.
Just me and my baby.
I'll move to London.
I'll never come back.

    I don't care what you do Gwen Ann.
    You are nothing to me.
    Go back to the *New Inn*.
    Go find your correspondent.

I don't want his body.
He got an old body.
You'd be surprised about him.
If I was to tell you.

    Would I?

I expect you know him.
I expect you seen him around.
You'd know him.
If I was to tell you.

    It don't matter.
    You are nothing to me.
    I don't want to know.
    I don't care.
    You got a cheek coming here.
    This is private.
    This is my house.
    Nobody asked you.
    You must have come looking.

I did.
I'm not ashamed.
I want you.
I want you for what you can give me.

    That's all right isn't it?
    But it goes two ways.
    And I don't want you.
    I been a father already.
    I had enough.

I don't want you here.

You are rubbish.

Part of you is rubbish.

With them words hurting her deep. Watching her get that handbag together and gloves. Looking smart as any woman you can see in Ponty. And a lot prettier. Except you definitely cannot stand her in that bedroom. With your mood a thousand miles away from her kind of talking.

Part of you is rubbish too.

The selfish part I mean.

That is big rubbish.

You are mostly rubbish.

You smash things up.

You empty people.

I got one life Gwen Ann.

You had a piece.

That's all.

And she brushes past you all of a huff out on to the landing without saying nothing more. And you follow her down to the front door. And she just stares into the street where it all looks pretty slushy and drab. Telling her

You got no right.

But she don't say anything not one word. Watching her pick through the pavement snow on to the road. And this shape in the doorway further down the street catching your eye just for an instant as she walks past out of sight. Just this shape you can hardly tell is a person except for one slight movement there in the shadows. Maybe just a leg shifting about. Maybe just a shoulder. But there is someone there watching you.

So you stare. And you squint. But the distance and the wind and the night don't let you see who is in the doorway. Making you call out

Melody?

Melody?

Is that you there?

Stepping slow down them slippery front steps. Not taking your eyes from that shadow. Feeling for the edge of the gutter with your foot and stepping into the slush. Standing there staring across the road feeling this cold seep all through your feet. Not caring about that.

Hearing this lorry rumbling near to your left coming down the street. Letting it pass in a squelch and squirt driving on sidelights. Reading Replacement Cleaners on the side. Then staring hard at the doorway. But the person is gone. The leg and the shoulder have gone on down Wood Street in a silent trot through the snow. And you can hardly tell standing there facing the wind what person it was. Except there is a gentleness to the way that figure runs. There is a care taken. There is a certain balance and a movement to the shape. And you can hardly tell that it is a woman.

Melody?

Stop for me.

Is that you?

But you got nothing to go on. Nothing more than a feeling. And your shouting is lost to the wind. It is blown back down your throat. There is no loudness to your voice. And the words you say and the name that you call are broken by the cold.

[25]

With them day-to-day ordinary things being done or forgotten by Sunday so it don't matter if there is dinner in the cupboard or a chain on the upstairs flush. Nor any of the things you got to answer in letters or call in about next time you are in Ponty. Nor whether them laundry boys have dumped your stuff out the back lane cubby-hole again so they get damp and got to be aired. Nor whether it is eight o'clock or ten o'clock or early afternoon. It don't matter on Sunday.

Waking slow and finding you don't have to dress nor make up the bed on account of dropping off where you flopped across the eiderdown the night before. And being pleased about that.

Hearing some dogs barking half-hearted in the distance. And the faint sound of a snare drummer girl practising fanatical up in Oaklands maybe or on some rostrum in the sky. But then nothing else. No other sounds. There is no voice outside in the street. And you reckon it must be early. Staring at your watch and seeing it is still half-past eleven from the night before. Shaking the thing and seeing the second hand go forward a few ticks.

Tick-tocking your life away O my lamb.

Where will you spend eternity?

    I got plans Lord.

I heard that one before O my lamb.

You got eff all plans isn't it.

I knows everything I do.

Wondering about that good Lord going around everywhere saying all them creepy things even before you got yourself together in the senses so early in the day. And you reckon it is on account of Sunday that he have come around clocking everybody just so they remember it is his day set aside for worshipping him and adoring him and glorifying that special name he got same as Ieuan Watts is always prattling on about.

I got plans for making plans.

For making things straight Lord.

One day I will get a plan going.

    One day you will be part of my plan O lamb.

What you got in mind Lord?

Is there a pit in Heaven?

    There are many pits.

    There are many workers.

    They toil.

Toil?

    It is happy work.

    You will not mind the work.

    There is no muck.

    There is no sweat.

    There is no cold.

    Neither shall ye hunger nor thirst.

When I got my plan going I will say.

    I will be listening O my lamb.

    I will wait.

Pressing that Fidelity button and hearing the pips for nine o'clock. Putting your watch right and switching off the news. Thinking as how you could get across to Glyntaff before dinner showing some kind of respect for the dead and Rachel and Miriam. And pleasing the good Lord who is clocking you and adding up your score. And knowing as how you are definitely low on points lately if spreading happiness around gets good marks.

Rolling off that bed stiff as pokers and feeling this shoe in your jacket pocket. Reckoning it must be Beano's by the look of the size hardly longer than a fag packet. Being nearly new and a mystery for ever as to how you ever got hold of it. Chucking that item into his porch as you pass through the pavement slush down Wood Street where new-laid milk bottles line both sides same as sentries guarding delicate bellies fast asleep upstairs.

Down King's Hill past Frank Troy's garage where they had your car a week nearly since the differential sprung loose. Making you think as how you might swap the Avenger for a Viva when the time is right. Maybe a yellow one with a black roof. Something fresh. Something with the taste of spring. Something no man ever owned before.

And onto the main road where there is no snow nor slush only orange grit and sand and salt. Making it easier to walk on that road than the pavement stunk up and banked with grime and yesterday's offering. All the way to Cemetery Road round the sickle bend where some kind of wire meshings back the rock falls famous for killing ape-minded kids when the holidays come. And into Glyntaff through them big green gates. Making new footprints in snow as fresh as the hour it fell.

Towards the far end where Rachel and Miriam got their plots in the shadow of Paradise Hill. Feeling the soles of your shoes crunching on the marble gravel just covered by the snow. Passing hundreds of gravestones mostly neglected. With withered stalks from tulips and carnations or hyacinths higgledy-piggledy drooping brown and black and dead from out of their squat little pots.

In memoriam. In remembrance. Side by side. In memory of our loving son. In memory of our loving daughter. To Mum. Dad. October nineteen forty Eric (and a marble anchor). Death shall have no dominion (lies all lies). Till we meet again. Rest in peace. Peace. Mam July seventeenth nineteen sixty-nine thirty-two Velindre. Peter ten years eight months Velindre. Perfect peace Annie sixty-two Velindre. Rest from thy labours Dad and Mam and Michael and Joan and Elizabeth and Gran and Blackie July nineteen seventy-five autoroute Narbonne. Dai nineteen forty (and a small stone soldier leaning on a small stone Lee-Enfield head bowed). Herbert Isaac Price eighteen sixty-three to December twenty-fourth nineteen sixty-six a well run race.

With maybe no more than six or seven others same as yourself picking out around the cemetery. Getting about their own private business while they got the chance. Some of them holding trowels for scraping moss from stones. And one filling a milk bottle with drips from a frozen tap.

Got to keep up appearances.

Got to keep the headstone smart.

She chose it herself.

Always was a bit previous.

Chose white marble.

Matt finish.

Gold lettering.

Green gravel chippings.

Anything to be awkward.

Always needs cleaning.

Attracts the moss.

Attracts the dirt.

Look at it again.

Only did it last month.

Chose white marble.

Matt finish.

I ask you.

Look at it again.

Bloody silly bitch.

Rot there you cow.

To where it says Rachel and Miriam. With them plots looking pretty spruced now that burial board have dug in the rose bushes they promised. And the flatness of the snow above their private turf telling you as how the earth have settled tidy on top of them coffins. And as how they are long dead. And definitely of the past. Feeling nothing much except a piece of sad and a shiver for the way it finished. Not caring why. Nor even wondering. Though you know when the spring have come you will put flowers in them pots. That you will brush up the plaque. And trim off the turf. That you will want to do that.

Walking back from Glyntaff down the Broadway where just a few chimneys are smoking blue. Watching the streamers curl upwards unshoved by the wind. With the sky not promising but dry until dinner you think.

Round Taff Street past True Form into Ynysangharad Park where the snowfall is patchy now and melting away along a thousand rough channels inevitably towards the river.

Standing on the footbridge staring at the mighty swirl. Hearing that frothed up gurgle as the Rhondda meets the Taff across the dinosaur's back sleeping for ever midstream. And thinking as how one of them passing strangers might remember that sound when the time is right. When the mood is just so. For sometimes that sound is like laughter. And sometimes it is like crying.

I thought it was you.

Had your shape isn't it.

So I come to tell you.

    Is that right?

She is mine.

And I love her.

    They said she was back.

And she don't want you.

She don't want to see you.

She had a guts full of this running away.

    There was no need.

    Never saw the point.

She done it.

Her and the boy.

And now they are back.

So you keep away mister.

You had your go isn't it.

You are nothing special.

She won't be looking for you.

Be told Ben.

There is no next time.

I could kill you both.

And the way he says them words tells you as how he have been thinking of killing for a very long time. Like he have come to a decision deep inside his mind. And his eyes look black. And they give you the willies. And he knows what he is saying.

If there is a next time I will.

I will Ben.

 What's all this talk of killing?

 You don't have to say kill.

 Melody come back to you.

 It's over for me and her.

Too bloody royal mister.

You listen what I'm saying.

Keep your dick out of her.

And he is gone away over the footbridge onto his side of the river. Calling two big mongrels to heel as he rounds the True Form shoe window out of sight.

Hearing old Saint Catherine gong out eleven o'clock to any head half-awake for counting. Half-awake for caring in this Sunday morning-after-the-night-before town. Wondering about the Deep Maritime and the afternoon shift starting at two with hardly a totful of men for weighing down them skiffs. Being always the same on Sunday and a fact that bloody Coal Board got to live with. Except today you reckon there is a distinct chance they might get the benefit of your labour for eight hours at least. There is every hope you might be there at two. There is you could say reason for believing. A definite possibility.